You're out of line

But Dougal couldn't touching her.

The air vibrated between them. The erotic promise buried in their kiss made him shudder.

His need for her went beyond all reason. He'd never felt anything like this. He should escape while he could, but then she pulled away and whispered, "Would you like to come back to my room?"

No, no, say no.

But his stupid tongue did not obey. She was pulling him headlong into her fantasy. What he said was, "There's nothing I'd enjoy more."

She unlocked the door, flicked on the light, drew him inside the room with her.

Then she captured his mouth with hers again.

That was all it took to convince him that his decision had been the right one. Testosterone surged through his body. His muscles tightened. His hands roved over her lush curves and he dipped his head to deepen their kiss.

This was so unlike him—losing control, losing his head. And yet he couldn't deny the power of this attraction. It was crazy and scary as hell, but it was too real to deny. His muscles ached. His skin burned.

Beyond all reason, he had to have her.

Blaze™

Dear Reader,

Have you ever wanted to cut loose and do something wild and crazy even if it's not in your nature, simply to see how the other half lives?

Well, that's what happens to good girl Roxanne Stanley when she finds herself recruited as a corporate spy by her boss. Her mission: find out exactly what goes on at Eros Airlines and Fantasy Resorts and report back to him. Roxie's not keen on subterfuge, but she's got a kid sister to put through college, and the promotion her boss dangles in front of her is too tempting to ignore. But what Roxie doesn't count on are the sexual fantasies provoked by the erotic resort and one very sexy tour guide, aka our handsome hero, Dougal Lockhart, an undercover security expert! It's not long before Roxie lands at the top of his suspects list *and* becomes the woman who drives him wild!

I hope you enjoy *Zero Control*. Don't forget to tell your friends about the wonderful stories you can find between the pages of a Harlequin novel. Visit me at www.loriwilde.com.

Much love,

Lori Wilde

Lori Wilde

ZERO CONTROL

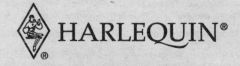

TORONTO • NEW YORK • LONDON
AMSTERDAM • PARIS • SYDNEY • HAMBURG
STOCKHOLM • ATHENS • TOKYO • MILAN • MADRID
PRAGUE • WARSAW • BUDAPEST • AUCKLAND

Recycling programs
for this product may
not exist in your area.

ISBN-13: 978-0-373-79510-9

ZERO CONTROL

Copyright © 2009 by Laurie Vanzura.

www.eHarlequin.com

Printed in U.S.A.

ABOUT THE AUTHOR

Lori Wilde is the author of forty books. She's been nominated for a RITA® Award and four *Romantic Times BOOKreviews* Reviewers' Choice Awards. Her books have been excerpted in *Cosmopolitan*, *Redbook* and *Quick & Simple*. Lori teaches writing online through Ed2go. She's an R.N. trained in forensics, and she volunteers at a battered women's shelter.

Books by Lori Wilde

HARLEQUIN BLAZE

*The White Star
**The Martini Dares
***Perfect Anatomy
†Uniformly Hot!

Don't miss any of our special offers. Write to us at the following address for information on our newest releases.

Harlequin Reader Service
U.S.: 3010 Walden Ave., P.O. Box 1325, Buffalo, NY 14269
Canadian: P.O. Box 609, Fort Erie, Ont. L2A 5X3

To Kathryn Lye,
who always makes me look good.

1

"YOUR AGENCY HAS THE JOB, but only under one condition."

Taylor Milton Corben, owner and CEO of Eros Airlines and Fantasy Adventure Vacations, folded her arms and leveled a look at former Air Force Captain Dougal Lockhart. Taylor was a sophisticated redhead with chic blond highlights threaded through her stylish hair, unwavering chocolate brown eyes and dynamite legs. She was also the new wife of Dougal's best friend, Daniel Corben.

Dougal drew himself up to his full six-foot-two-inch height and held Taylor's steady gaze. He should have known there would be a catch. In his experience, there was always a catch.

Did her stipulation have anything to do with the reason he'd left the military and started his own private duty air marshal service? Daniel had probably told her what had happened to him in Germany. Instinctively Dougal stuck his hand in his pants pocket and ran his fingertips over the 9mm slug fragment that he'd had turned into a key chain precisely so he wouldn't forget. The bullet scar at his upper right thigh—at the very same level as his pocket—throbbed at the memory.

Dougal steeled himself for a proviso he couldn't live with, but he wasn't in any position to be choosy. He needed the work. He was trying to get his fledgling business off the ground and it was a struggle. Last month he'd been forced to take out a loan just to make payroll. But there were some things he simply wouldn't do. No matter how badly he needed the money.

"What's the condition?" He fisted his hands.

"I want you and your team to go undercover—"

"That's a given."

She ignored his interruption and went on smoothly. "As tour guides."

"Tour guides?" She caught him off guard with that one.

"Tour guides," she repeated.

"Why?"

"I need you and your men not just on my planes, but at my resorts, as well." She leaned back in her chair, crossed her legs and angled her head to size him up.

"The Lockhart Agency is an air marshal service, not resort security," he said.

"Should I take that to mean you don't want the job?"

Dammit, he did want the job and she was well aware of it. At least she hadn't made any reference to Germany or Ava. He shifted his weight, his feet shoulder-width apart, hands resting on his hips.

Taylor laughed. "You look like an old West gun-slinging sheriff staving off a lynch mob, Dougal. Relax, have a seat."

He forced himself to drop his arms by his sides and settle into the plush leather couch across from Taylor's expensive mahogany desk. He did have a tendency to brace for battle even when there was nothing to brace for.

"What does the job entail?" he asked.

"You'll work for the entire first two weeks in May," she said. "It's a fourteen-day tour."

He nodded. "No problem there."

"You and your men will take tour guide training with the rest of my employees. You've got four men. We have four new tours starting next month and I want air marshals on all the planes and at the facilities."

"Okay," he said cautiously. "What else?"

"You'll be required to wear costumes."

"Excuse me?"

"I'm sorry, but it's nonnegotiable." Taylor might look like a pampered supermodel, but she was a sharp business woman. "In fact, if you decide to take the job, you should start growing your beard now."

"Beard?" Involuntarily his hand went up to stroke his jaw. He'd never worn facial hair in his life.

"You'll be playing the Bard."

"Who?"

"Shakespeare."

Dougal frowned. "I'm not following you."

"I'm concerned that the saboteur is targeting the Romance of Britannia tour next, and the lead tour guide on that junket dresses as Shakespeare. Or rather the *Shakespeare in Love* version of what he dressed like."

"Why are you so sure the saboteur is targeting that particular tour?"

Taylor opened up her desk, took out a green file folder and passed it across her desk. Dougal opened it and read the letter inside.

You thought those little incidents at your Venice resort was trouble? You haven't seen anything yet, bitch. Just wait until one of your planes falls from the sky. Wouldn't that set tongues wagging? Do you have any idea how vulnerable your air fleet is? Just take a look.

Attached to the anonymous letter was a schematic of the inside of a Bombardier CRJ200. In the margins, written in red, was a detailed listing of the numerous ways a saboteur could cripple the private jet.

His blood chilled.

Dougal raised his head and met Taylor's gaze. For the first time, he saw real fear in her eyes and he was strangely comforted. If she was afraid, that meant she was taking the threats seriously, and the fact that she'd laid her cards on the table made him feel instantly calmer. He was the kind of guy who liked to have a map of the quicksand bogs before he ventured into the jungle. "What did the police say when you showed them the note?"

Taylor plowed a hand through her hair. "I didn't."

"Why not?"

"I don't want any more negative publicity than I've already gotten. I prefer to keep this in-house."

"We should have it dusted for prints."

"I already sent it out to a private lab. There were dozens of prints on the envelope, none on the letter beyond mine and the temp who's been filling in since my executive assistant decided not to return from maternity leave."

"What happened in Venice?"

Taylor inhaled audibly. "A few months back my Venice resort experienced a series of…problems."

"Meaning?"

"Malfunctioning smoke alarms that allowed a fire in the laundry room to go undetected until it had done several thousand dollars' worth of damage. It was suspicious because the smoke alarms had just passed inspection the week before."

"Cause of the blaze?"

"Undetermined."

"Go on."

"After one of the scheduled banquet feasts, a few guests contracted food poisoning, sending them to the hospital for treatment. And finally a Renoir was stolen. The security system had been turned off, and the police suspected an inside job. I fired the manager, hired someone new. Taken one by one it seemed like mere coincidence, but then I learned an exposé reporter was following me."

"The incident between you and Daniel in Spain," he said.

"Yes." She nodded. "Once the reporter aired his piece, I thought the sabotage was all over. Apparently—" she waved at the letter Dougal was still holding "—I was wrong, and the guy was just lying in wait, lulling me into a false sense of security."

"You believe it's a man?"

She shrugged. "Aren't men usually the ones who do these kinds of things?"

Dougal thought of Ava. "Not necessarily."

Taylor pulled her lips back in a pensive expression. "I hadn't considered a woman."

"What makes you think this saboteur is going to strike the Romance of Britannia tour?"

"That diagram is not just any generic Bombardier schematic. It was torn from the handbook of the plane that services that specific tour." She pulled the handbook from her desk and tossed it to him.

Dougal opened it to the back where the schematics were located and saw the jagged edges where the paper had been ripped out. It didn't take a crime scene investigator to see that the torn segments matched. "Any clue as to who could be behind this?"

She shook her head. "I'm no stranger to controversy, you know that. There have been outspoken religious fundamentalists picketing my resorts, condemning them as hedonistic and wicked. Then there are the superkinky customers who threaten to sue me because Eros refuses to fulfill their illegal fantasies. My competitors are jealous of the way I've taken my father's dated commuter airline model and given it a very profitable new millennium makeover. But many on the board of directors are unhappy about this new direction. Making enemies is all part of doing business in the tourism industry."

"This feels more personal." He fingered the torn pages. "For one thing, how did they get access to the jet's handbook?"

"I don't know. That's where you come in."

"I'm not sure how my men are going to like dressing up and playing tour guide."

"I understand it's asking a lot. I'm willing to sweeten the deal." She named a figure so high it was all Dougal could do not to blink in disbelief. "What do you say?"

He smiled. "How can I refuse?"

Taylor reached across the desk, rested her hand on Dougal's forearm. "I want this person caught and I want my guests kept safe."

"We'll take care of it."

"I'm counting on you."

He got to his feet, thought about what happened in Germany and swallowed hard. He could do this. He had to do this. He'd learned from his past. He wouldn't be played for a fool again. He met Taylor's steady gaze and made her a promise. "You can depend on me. I won't let you down."

At that moment, a knock sounded on the door and before Taylor could say, "Come in" the door opened and a heavyset older gentleman, with a straight-shouldered military bearing, stepped over the threshold.

Immediately, Dougal saluted the former general who had once been his superior officer. "General Miller, sir."

"Please." The general waved his hand. "There's no need for that. We're both retired."

Dougal relaxed his stance.

"How are you, Uncle Chuck?" Taylor asked and got up to give the general a kiss on his cheek.

"I'm just fine, princess." He wrapped an arm around her waist.

"How's Aunt Mitzi?"

"Blowing through all my money on a spa day with her friends."

He grinned at her, and then looked at Dougal. "Are you in the middle of something here? I thought I'd take you to lunch and you could tell me what's going on with that sabotage business."

"Actually, I just hired Dougal and his team to augment my security staff. I just received another threatening letter. This one targeting my air fleet."

"Oh?" The general canted his head.

"I've started my own private air marshal service, sir," Dougal explained.

"Ah." Miller nodded. "Applying the lessons you learned about security after that mess in Germany."

Was that a personal dig? The man's tone made Dougal squirm in memory over what had happened. "Yes. And I'm going to do everything in my power to ensure that Eros Air stays safe."

"See that you do," Miller said curtly. "See that you do."

"HEY, HANDSOME, YOU CAN SHAKE your spear over here anytime you want."

In light of that sexy remark, Dougal forced himself not to roll his eyes as a group of women filed onto the Bombardier CRJ200, chatting, giggling and finding their seats. The majority of them were young, rich and attractive. The red-haired woman who'd cracked the suggestive comment briefly met his gaze, then lowered her eyelashes, licked her lips and murmured, *"Yummm-o,"* before moving down the aisle.

It didn't help matters that Dougal was dressed like Joseph Fiennes from *Shakespeare in Love* right down to the artsy, beatnik beard he was itching to shave.

After all, this was Eros Airlines and Fantasy Adventure Vacations and Taylor's company's catch phrase was Something Sexy in the Air. Other than the pilot and copilot, who were both pushing sixty, Dougal was the only male employee aboard. He felt like the last cut of prime beef in the meat market on the Fourth of July.

He was going to have to talk to Taylor. The puffy-sleeved shirt and skintight leather breeches were bad enough, but the facial hair simply had to go. Resisting the urge to scratch his jaw, Dougal greeted each guest with the requisite smile, welcoming them aboard with an affected British accent. It was going to be a long two weeks.

Look at the side benefits. You stand an excellent chance of getting laid.

Except he and his men had signed a contract with a morality clause. While they were encouraged to flirt with the guests, sexual contact was strictly prohibited. Dougal watched a provocative young woman with a great ass wiggle away and he hissed out his breath.

Damn that morality clause.

That was the moment Dougal spotted her.

The last one to board.

The one who didn't belong.

She stood out like a single red rose in a field full of dandelions, all genteel and otherworldly, an escapee from the pages of *Grimm's Fairy Tales.* He half expected to see unicorns and songbirds and butterflies trailing after her.

Her hair was raven's-wing black, her skin pure alabaster, her eyes a stunning shade of ice-floe blue. She must be wearing contact lenses; no one's eyes were that color naturally. She was dressed in a butter-yellow sundress made out of some soft, frothy material that caused his mouth to water. Dougal could taste the sugar-coated marshmallow bunnies and chickens his mother had put in his Easter basket when he was a kid.

Unbidden, he found himself imagining what she looked like underneath that springtime sundress. Did she have on white cotton panties with a sensible underwire bra? Or would he find a delightful surprise? Maybe a wicked scarlet bustier and G-string panties?

Dougal tilted his head. No, he decided. Pink satin tap pants and a matching camisole. Sweet yet sassy. A good girl longing for adventure but nervous about reaching out and grabbing what she desired.

And yet it was more than her ethereal beauty that set her apart from the others, and Dougal was trained to notice subtle differences. It was the serious, "all-business" slant to her slender shoulders and the determined set to her chin, as if she had something to prove. It was the perceptive expression in her eyes, the purposeful way she moved and the manner in which she was sizing him up just as intensely as he was measuring her.

No mere vacationer, this one. Not a woman simply looking for a good time. This enigmatic lady had an agenda.

Alarm bells went off in his head. Until he knew exactly what her agenda was, Dougal was keeping a close eye on her.

Another thing that didn't fit—she was traveling solo. Everyone else on the vacation had traveling companions, but this mysterious miss appeared to be all alone. No doting husband or fiancé or boyfriend at her elbow. No best buddy yapping her ear off. No mother or sister or cousin.

Perhaps she also worked for Eros, maybe she was an actress paid to help set the stage for the Romance of Britannia tour the group was embarking upon and it was her first day on the job. If you put her in historical garb along the lines of the ridiculous outfit he'd been forced to wear, she'd be a shoo-in.

Except that Taylor hadn't told him about any new employees joining the group, and he'd made it quite clear that he was to be kept in the loop regarding anything to do with passenger safety. Odd, though, that while his brain and experience were warning him to watch out for her, his gut was telling him something startling and stupid.

She's the one you've been waiting for.

Why the hell was he giving himself mixed messages? The last time this had happened he'd ended up with a bullet in his thigh.

The woman reached the top step of the metal mobile stairs and their eyes met. Quickly she glanced at his outfit and when her gaze found his again, a slight grin tipped her lips. She was laughing at him.

He cocked an eyebrow, gave her his best Joe Cool expression and stretched out his hand. "Welcome to Eros Airlines, where *your* pleasure is our only concern."

The greeting might have been prescribed, but the emphasis was all his. Dougal didn't know why he extended his hand as she stepped into the cabin. He hadn't shaken any of the other women's hands. Impulse motivated. That bothered him because he struggled so hard to control his impulses.

For the longest moment she said nothing, merely stood there staring at his outstretched hand. It was damned unnerving.

"Hello," she murmured in a husky, breathy voice, and then turned her back on him and started down the aisle.

"Wait," he said and touched her shoulder, stopping her. *Hold up, you're coming on too strong. You don't want to blow your cover.* "What's your name?"

She turned back, raised an eyebrow. "My name?"

Why was she being so cryptic? Did she have something to hide or was he too hypervigilant?

"For our exemplary customer service." He blurted the first excuse that came into his head and manufactured what he hoped was an earnest smile. "We didn't earn our five-star rating by calling our guests 'Hey You.'"

There it was again, that sly, amused grin, as if she found him extremely comical. "I'm Roxanne Stanley. But my friends call me Roxie."

"Roxie." He extended his hand again.

"You're assuming we're going to be friends."

"Not assuming, just hoping."

The minute their palms touched, a shudder shot straight down his spine. His stomach squeezed and his balls pulled up tight against his body and he was just...*rocked*.

The intensity of his reaction disturbed him. Resolutely he shook off the feeling. By nature he was a guarded man. It was the way he'd been born—cautious, cagey, always on the lookout for trouble, seeing the world though the eyes of a troubleshooter. Life circumstances had added to his innate wall, one emotional brick at a time. The one time he'd opened himself up, let down his guard, chipped a few bricks off the wall and—*wham!*

His old bullet wound ached at the thought. *Fool me once, shame on you. Fool me twice, shame on me.*

"And you are..." Roxie tilted her head.

"Here to make your every fantasy come true."

"Ah," she said. "Is that so?" Her smile widened to reveal a double dimple deep in her left cheek. God, he'd always been a sucker for dimples, and look here, she had two.

Key word being sucker. *Keep your testosterone in check, Lockhart. You're on the job.*

"Let's see where you're sitting." Dougal leaned closer, ostensibly to read her boarding pass, but he already knew where she was sitting. He'd memorized the passenger manifest, and he recalled that Ms. Stanley was seated in the first row, near the window, while he had the aisle seat beside her. Handy coincidence.

What he really wanted was to see how she'd react to his proximity. Would she flirt like a single woman on a sexy vacation retreat? Or would she act guilty like someone up to no good?

When it came down to it, she did neither.

Instead, with an unflappable expression, Roxanne Stanley said silkily, "You're blocking my way, Mr. Fantasy Man. Now if you'll excuse me..."

He moved aside, but the passageway was small and he was

large. She had to squeeze past him to get to her seat and in the
process her hip grazed his upper thigh. It was the slightest
contact, barely there, and yet Dougal's cock stirred instantly
inside those damned leather breeches as surely as if she'd
stroked him.

This was crazy. He didn't lose control like this, not with so
little provocation. He took a deep breath, trying to cool his
heated blood. Wanting a woman—hell, who was he kidding,
he was *craving* her—brought risks and vulnerabilities.

*Think about something else. Whatever you do, do not watch
her ass as she walks away.*

The woman moved past him and his gaze homed in on her
ass like a heat-seeking missile. She swiveled her head and
caught him staring. Her steal-your-breath blue eyes locked onto
his and sucked the air right out of his lungs.

In that moment it was as if they were totally alone on the
airplane. The noise of dozens of voices humming in conversation faded away and Dougal's focus narrowed to only her.

Her gaze was steady, but he saw a faint tinge of pink color
her cheeks and she lowered those long, thick black lashes. His
heart knocked. She looked at once strong and extremely vulnerable, and he wondered what secrets she was keeping.

Had she been sent by one of Taylor's enemies? An irate
stockholder or a competitor? Or was it a personal agenda? Was
it revenge against Taylor? Was she a straitlaced saboteur deeply
offended by Eros Airlines and its sexually adventuresome vacations, or was he totally off the mark about her altogether?

Dougal couldn't deny that his instincts were telling him she
wasn't what she seemed, but did he trust his powers of deduc-
tive reasoning? Getting close to her was the only way to find
out, but something told him if he flew too near the flame of her
hot blue eyes he was going to get singed.

He clenched his teeth to keep from scooping her into his

arms and carrying her away to some secluded corner of the expensively decorated airplane and stripping off her clothes in a hungry effort to discover if her flesh tasted as sweet as it looked. He wanted to cup his palm around her breasts, to thread his fingers through that mane of lush black hair, to press his mouth against her ripe, rich lips.

"Is there something you need?" she asked.

You.

"No," he answered mildly.

He could almost hear her heart thumping, could feel his own heart slamming against his chest.

"Okay, then."

"Okay." Behind him, the flight attendant closed the door, but he didn't look away.

Roxie broke their stare. Ducking her head, she scurried toward her fully reclining, plush leather seat beside the window. Leaving Dougal feeling as if he was flying into the eye of a storm, and his instrument panel had just frizzed out.

2

ROXIE'S BOSS, PORTER LANGLEY, the owner and founder of Getaway Airlines, had seriously underestimated Taylor Corben. Roxie doubted that Porter realized how much money the woman lavished on her airline, nor did he have any idea that she was hiring gorgeous macho men as tour guides. Of course, that was the very reason Mr. Langley had sent her on this trip—to get the lowdown on Eros. Her boss hungered to follow in Taylor Corben's footsteps and open his own destination resort in Ireland, along the lines of Eros's version in Stratford.

The lavishness of the accommodations was the first item going into her report, after she got her hands to stop sweating and her pulse to quit pounding, following her encounter with the hunk in Renaissance attire. The way "Shakespeare" had stared at her caused Roxie to fear that he'd guessed her secret.

She was a mole.

Roxie hadn't been happy about the whole go-spy-on-the-competition assignment her boss had cooked up, but she was loyal to the bone when it came to people who'd given her a break, plus she desperately wanted the head of public relations position that her boss had dangled in front of her. Pulling off this little piece of corporate espionage would cinch her promotion.

The job was not only one she coveted, but the bump in salary would also allow her to put her kid sister, Stacy, through college. Roxie didn't want Stacy to end up like her, forced by circumstances and lack of money to give up on her dreams of becoming an actress.

She peered out the window. Even though she worked for an airline she wasn't a comfortable flyer, and heading to London twisted her stomach. Crossing miles and miles of ocean held little appeal.

She blew out her breath, ran her palms over the front of her thighs and then dug her BlackBerry from her purse to distract herself. She started to type in her impression of the big man in the Shakespeare costume and the lavish interior of the plane—mahogany wood paneling, cocktail bar at the back of the plane with a gleaming granite countertop, opulent carpeting—but then he came over and strapped himself into the last empty seat on the plane.

The seat right beside hers.

Unnerved, Roxie shut off her BlackBerry and returned it to her designer knockoff handbag she'd picked up at a yard sale. She definitely did not fit with this crowd, but her childhood had taught her to be someone else whenever she was in a dicey situation. Slip under the skin of an invented character. For the duration of this trip she was a smart, sharp, infinitely calm, corporate spy. She just had to keep reminding herself of that.

Inhaling, she caught a whiff of his spicy, masculine cologne and felt herself come undone. Fear revved her pulse rate. *Did* he suspect she was not typical of Eros's well-heeled clientele?

Play the game. Be the role.

To boost her confidence, she reached up to run her fingers over the gold-and-silver comedy-tragedy mask necklace she always wore. It was the last gift her parents had given her before they were killed two weeks after her eighteenth birthday.

"Hello, again." His deep voice rumbled, rolling over her ears like a gathering storm.

She felt something shake loose in her chest, a tearing-away

sensation like a boat breaking free from its mooring and drifting out to sea.

Be cool. You are an expert spy. Think Mata Hari, Antonia Ford, Belle Boyd.

"Hi," she said casually.

"I'm Dougal, by the way. Dougal Lockhart. Sorry about stonewalling you earlier. It's part of the flirtatious role-playing Eros requires from tour guides."

Role-playing she understood. It was how a shy girl from Albany made it in New York City. "So I deduced. Are you sitting here for the entire flight?"

Oh, damn, her voice had come out high and reedy.

"Yep. Does that distress you?"

"You're the one who should be distressed," she countered. When she'd first started working for Porter he'd coached her on how to go on the offensive diplomatically whenever she found herself backed into a corner, but the skill didn't come easily. By nature she was open, expressive, a people pleaser, and she had to fight against her tendency to be overly accommodating. It was only when she pretended to be someone else that she was able to change her behavior.

"Oh?" He cocked his head.

"I gotta warn you," Roxie amended. "I'm a nervous flyer. I get fidgety."

"And yet you're traveling alone."

"I am."

"Vacationing by yourself?"

Was he fishing for details? Fear hopscotched through her and she dug her fingernails into her palm. "What's wrong with that?"

"Nothing. It's brave."

"I like traveling alone," she lied. "I'm accountable to no one's agenda but my own."

"Touché." His gaze skimmed over the naked ring finger of her left hand. "I take it you're not married."

"Astute conclusion."

"Snarky." His eyes twinkled. "Unexpected but engaging."

"I'm happy I could provide you with some free entertainment." She took a peek at his ring finger. "You don't look married, either."

"Astute conclusion."

"Now you're just mocking me."

"Trying to keep your mind off takeoff."

"I appreciate the effort."

"If it would help any, feel free to grab hold of my arm," Dougal invited.

She dropped a glance at his strong forearm, poking from the rolled-up sleeves of his puffy white shirt. His forearms were ropy with muscles and thick, dark hair. She curled her fingers into fists and forced herself to breath normally.

"I've got to warn you, I tend to babble when I'm nervous." She scrunched her shoulder blades together.

"Babble away."

"You're too kind."

"Not at all. I have earplugs."

She had to laugh. Strange as it seemed, she was having fun. The plane taxied from the gate.

"Quick," Roxie said. "Say something to distract me. Take-offs and landings freak me out the most. That and looking out the window when we're over water."

"Looking out the window freaks you out?"

"Sort of."

"So why the window seat?"

"Because looking out the window keeps me from feeling claustrophobic."

"You're claustrophobic, too?"

"Only when I feel closed in."

He laughed again, the corners of his brown eyes crinkling. "You're funny."

"I'm happy that you find my terror amusing."

"It is a seven-hour flight. I have to take my amusement where I can find it." The teasing expression in his eyes warmed her from the inside out.

The plane rushed down the runway, gathering speed, the tarmac whizzing by in a gray-black blur. Roxie gripped the armrest.

Dougal held out his palm. "I'm here if you need a hand to hold on to."

Gratefully she took it, but the minute his fingers closed around hers, Roxie realized she'd made a grave mistake. His grip was firm, his palm calloused. His scent, a complicated aroma of spicy cologne, leather and sunshine invaded her nostrils.

Madness.

The plane was airborne, soaring.

Treetops fell away. Vehicles crawling along the freeway in rush-hour traffic glimmered like spotted stones. The early-morning sun burned orange against the clouds. Roxie jerked her gaze from the window to stare at the man beside her.

The warmth inside her kicked up to a sultry simmer. A labyrinth of emotions pummeled her. Overwhelmed, Roxie had to remind herself to breathe. What was going on here? Why was she feeling so…so…what was she feeling?

Attracted.

Yes, that was the word. She was attracted to him and the feeling scared her.

He held on tightly to her hand, and she closed her eyes so he couldn't read what she was struggling to hide.

The landing gear came up with a bump. Her eyes flew open. The sound never failed to send her heart lurching into her throat. Dougal squeezed her hand. A sexual tingle shot all the way up to her shoulder.

Think about something else.

But that was difficult to do, considering how delicious he smelled and how his quick-witted banter reminded her just how long it had been since she'd had sex.

Roxie tried to concentrate on the luxurious surroundings. The state-of-the-art flat-screen television sets at each seat were so sophisticated they'd make a techno geek weep with happiness. There were the elaborate meal menus that could send a gastronome into paroxysms of epicurean delight and the butter-soft, oversize leather chairs with enough legroom to satisfy the long-legged man beside her.

"How long have you been a tour guide?" She searched for something neutral to talk about, something that wouldn't inflame the feelings burning through her. Or result in her inadvertently giving herself away.

"I just started," Dougal explained. "In fact, this is my first trip."

"Really?"

"Yep."

"You seem so self-confident."

"It's all an act," he confided. "Inside, my knees are jelly."

"You fooled me."

"How so?"

"You don't look like you're scared of anything."

"Looks can be deceiving." The way he said it, the penetrating expression on his face made her feel as if he'd whipped off all her clothes and she was sitting there stark naked.

"What did you do before you took this job?" she asked.

"Variety of things."

"You seem a little old to still be finding yourself."

"Some of us are late bloomers."

"Late-blooming jelly knees? I'm not buying it."

He stroked his bearded chin. "No?"

"How old are you?"

"Thirty-three. You?"

"Anyone ever tell you it's impolite to ask a woman her age?"

"You brought up the topic," he pointed out.

"I guess I did. How old do you think I am?"

"That's so not fair. If I guess that you're older than you are, then you'll never speak to me again and that would be such a shame because you're definitely a woman worth speaking to. So let's see. You're sixteen going on seventeen?"

Okay, so she was flattered. Roxie didn't get this kind of talk from men very often. Mainly because she avoided situations where such talk could spring. To be honest, she avoided men and any hint of romantic relationships, but she wasn't dumb. She knew it was part of his tour guide please-the-customer shtick, so she relented and let him off the hook. "I'm twenty-eight."

"And you've got your life all figured out?"

She shrugged. "I guess."

He reclined his seat, crossed his ankles. "What do you do for a living?"

"Executive assistant," she said, wanting to lie as little as possible.

"Is this your first trip to Europe?"

"Yes. You?"

"Been many times. Twelve years in the Air Force."

"I guess that's why you became a tour guide? You know your way around the world."

"I've been around the block a time or two." He narrowed his eyes, his smile turned wicked and for a moment he looked positively hawkish. A calculating raptor analyzing the habits of his prey just before he swooped in for the kill. Suddenly she felt like a field mouse who'd ventured too far from home. What on earth had made her believe she could pull off something like this?

"Do you like music?" he asked.

"Sure." She shrugged. *Act nonchalant, sophisticated.* "Doesn't everyone?"

"Not everyone. I ask because Eros Airlines has satellite radio piped in. Listening to music might help you relax."

He leaned over her to reach for the console containing the small flat-screen television. She tried not to notice that his broad chest was mere inches from her lap. He opened a drawer, pulled out a headset and handed it to her. "What do you want to hear? I'll dial it in for you. Rap, country, classic, pop? You name it, we've got it."

"Emocore," she said.

The corners of his mouth turned down in a surprised, "Who knew?" expression. "Seriously?"

"You got something against emocore?"

"Matter of fact it's my favorite, but I really don't like the emo label," he said.

"It's dumb, I know. Why don't they just call it poignant punk rock? Who are your favs?"

"Rites of Spring, Embrace, Gray Matter."

"Oh, oh, don't forget Fire Party and Moss Icon."

"What do you like about it?"

"Emo is so raw, you know. Primal." Roxie pressed her palms together. "But it's also deep and expressive and soulful." Some people thought the music was loud and chaotic, but to Roxie the sound represented a part of herself she was afraid to explore any other way. The part of her that longed to flaunt convention, throw back her head and just howl at the moon.

Dougal shook his head. "I wouldn't have pegged you for an emo fan."

"Same here."

They grinned at each other.

Dougal shifted in his seat, angling his body toward her. "Okay, so what's your favorite food?"

"Italian."

"Me, too. What dish do you like best? Lasagna?"

"Always a crowd-pleaser, but my hands-down fav is chicken Marsala."

"No kidding? It's my favorite, as well."

"Wine, mushrooms, chicken in cream. What's not to love?"

"I couldn't agree with you more."

"What's your favorite dessert?"

"Brownies."

"With nuts."

"Absolutely."

"Pecans or walnuts?"

"Either will do, but I like walnuts best."

Roxie narrowed her eyes. "You're just telling me what I want to hear. That's your job."

He grinned, shrugged. "I like seeing you smile."

"Ha! I knew it. Flatterer."

"Doesn't mean that I'm lying. Slap some Fugazi on the MP3 player. Whip up a batch of chicken Marsala. Promise walnut brownies for dessert. Sit you across from me and it's the stuff of dreams."

Sudden silence sprouted between them, and Roxie felt an anxiety of a wholly different kind. "You can let go now," she whispered.

"What?"

"My hand. May I have it back? We're in the air. My takeoff terror has passed."

"Oh, yeah, sure." He let go of her hand.

She dropped her hot, damp palm into her lap and averted her gaze. Her pulse galloped. "Thanks," she said. "You make a good distraction from fear of flying."

Now all I need is something to distract me from the distraction.

The captain turned off the Fasten Seat Belt sign, and Roxie, anxious to put as much distance between herself and Dougal as she could get, decided to visit the lavatory. A splash of cold water in her face to calm her racing pulse. She unbuckled her seat belt and got to her feet. "Excuse me, may I slip by you?"

Dougal moved his long legs into the aisle just as the plane lurched. Roxie hissed in her breath. The plane pitched again, thrusting her forward onto his lap. His arms closed around her, Roxie's fanny snugged against his thighs. She peered into his face, glanced away, and then looked back again.

Sharp, dark eyes stared straight into her, holding her motionless. "Are you okay?" he asked, his voice sounding husky and strange as if someone was tightening a wire around his throat.

"What was that?" she asked.

"Turbulence. It'll be fine."

A sudden stillness settled over her. She sighed deeply and all the air fled her lungs. She felt a million different things at once. Safe, desired, happy, confused. The shock of recognition passed through her. He was a stranger and yet it was as if she'd known him her entire life. How could that be?

In that split second of surprise, she felt as if she'd met her match, identified the other half of life's jigsaw puzzle. She was like a lost traveler, wandering in a foreign land, who'd stumbled upon a field of flowers indigenous to her homeland. No, not just the flowers of her homeland, but the same glorious mix that once grew in her own backyard. She gave no thought to whether he was friend or foe. Her impulse was simply to rush to the sweet smells of home.

Roxie's heart surged toward Dougal, and she knew in that moment she'd totally lost all control. How in the hell was she going to pull off corporate espionage when all she could think about was pulling off Dougal Lockhart's clothes?

"You can let go of me now," Roxie said.

Dougal loosened his grip, and she struggled to get to her feet. The plane lurched again sending her right back into his lap, and a small gasp of surprise escaped those perfect pink lips. He wrapped his arms around her waist again. "Maybe you should just sit tight until we get through this turbulence."

Even as he said it, he had to clench his teeth to fight off his stirring erection. Getting a boner with her on his lap might be totally natural, but he was certain it would alarm her. It alarmed him. He was supposed to be in charge of passenger safety on this plane, not coming on to a guest.

He took a deep breath and immediately inhaled her heavenly scent. Her delicate aroma encircled his nose, played havoc with his brain cells. The fragrance, coupled with her body heat, slicked his mind with desire and he couldn't think of anything but her.

Bad idea. *Okay, no more breathing.*

She wriggled in his lap, and Dougal swallowed a groan. This was crazy. He had to put a stop to it. "Um, maybe we should get you back into your seat."

"But you said—"

"Buckle you down tight. That's what you need. Buckled down." Why had he said that? Now he had an image of her, seat belt resting against her lower abdomen, the buckle right at the level of her—

Stop it!

Before she could feel the erection he could no longer control, Dougal transferred her quickly into her seat, settled back against his own chair, plucked a glossy magazine from the pouch on the side and plunked it into his lap as camouflage. He prayed she hadn't spied the overt evidence of his desire. He cast a glance over at her. She stared at him, wide-eyed.

His pulse jumped. Her gaze searched his face for a long

moment. Stunning blue eyes, full of innocence. She smiled coyly, lowered her gaze and then turned to look out the window.

What was that look all about?

The plane jerked, shuddered. Several of the other passengers gasped out loud. Roxie splayed a hand at the base of her throat.

He rested a palm on her shoulder. "You hanging in there?"

The tremulous glint in her eyes told him she was frightened, but the firm jut to her chin suggested she was toughing it out. Her vulnerability tugged at him.

"Are you sure it's just turbulence?" she whispered.

Until Roxie had asked the question, he was almost positive the lurching of the plane was nothing more than turbulence, but now she had aroused his suspicion. Could there be something amiss with the aircraft?

He thought of the death threats Taylor had received. Immediately his mind conjured disturbing scenarios. Taylor had hired him because she feared someone might tamper with the planes, and he'd agree with her that the possibility existed. To that end, he'd been with the pilot when he'd done his preflight check, and Dougal had personally searched the private jet, but he wasn't a mechanic. An expert saboteur could have rigged something up that neither he nor the pilot had detected.

The plane vibrated.

This time the collective let out more than just gasps.

Concern for passenger safety got Dougal's mind off his attraction to Roxie and back on his job. He unbuckled his seat belt and stood.

"Is something wrong? You look worried."

"I'm going to speak with the pilot about the turbulence." He gave her a reassuring smile.

"Thank you." She exhaled an audible sigh.

Dougal made his way up the aisle toward the cockpit. He was forced to pause and brace himself each time the plane pitched like a boat in a tropical squall. He tapped on the cabin door with a coded knock and the copilot let him in.

"Problems?" he asked, shutting the door behind him.

"Something's wrong with the autopilot," said the pilot, Nicholas Peters, a heavy-browed, stern-faced man with jowls that hinted at Russian ancestry. "Every time we try to switch over the plane pitches."

Uneasiness rippled over Dougal. "Any idea what's causing the glitch?"

Peters frowned, shook his head.

"Do you think someone could have tampered with the autopilot?" Dougal recalled the detailed schematics of the plane's electrical system that had accompanied the most threatening of Taylor's letters.

"It's not likely," Peters hedged. "I'm ninety-nine-percent sure it's nothing more than a stuck valve."

It was that one percent Dougal worried about. The pilot's reassurance didn't lessen the thread of anxiety pulling across his shoulder muscles. "Should we turn back?"

"Not necessary," said the copilot, Jim Donovan. "We can fly manually. We've already contacted the control tower and reported the problem. They gave us the thumbs-up to continue on to London. It just means Nick and I'll have to work a little harder on the transatlantic flight. But it's nothing we can't handle."

That might be true, but Dougal was calling Taylor when they got to England and having her put a team of mechanics on the Bombardier, just to make sure there'd been no sabotage. Yes, he might be overreacting, but it was better to be safe than sorry.

"To keep from alarming the passengers, we'll blame it on turbulence. I was just about to make the announcement when you came in," Peters said, and then he hit the button that allowed him to deliver the message throughout the cabin. "Ladies and gentleman, sorry for the bumpy ride. We've hit a bit of turbulence, but we're taking her up a few thousand feet, and all should be clear from here on out, so sit back and enjoy the ride."

"Let me know if anything comes up that needs my input," Dougal said.

"Will do." Peters nodded.

Dougal made his way back down the aisle. Roxie looked at him with eyes that could break a man's heart. He stood there for a moment as if held in place by a wire strung from the middle of his back into the plane's ceiling, staring back, blood thick as paint chugging through his veins.

"Everything's okay," he said, forcing himself to slide into the seat beside her once more and noticing she had a death grip on the armrest. "You can relax."

Take your own advice, Lockhart.

"Thanks for checking," she murmured. "I feel better now." Soft, light, feminine, seductive, she possessed the sexiest speaking voice he'd ever heard.

Do not start that again, stop being so aware of her.

Far easier said than done. She wasn't the kind of woman you could choose to ignore.

"No problem," he croaked.

"Not everyone would have taken the trouble to reassure me."

Dougal could hardly think. Talk about eye candy. Perfectly arched eyebrows the same bewitching ebony shade as her hair. Long, lush lashes. A straight, slender nose with delicate nostrils. Her strawberry colored lips tipped up in a slight smile. Fascinating.

He fisted his hands. Roxie wasn't for him. For one thing he had a job to do, and for all he knew she could be a saboteur. Never mind that she looked sweet and innocent. She'd probably be sweet and innocent in bed, as well, and who needed that kind of sex? He liked his women experienced and uninhibited when it came to lovemaking. He didn't fancy himself as anyone's teacher.

Who cares? You're not going to find out what she's like in the sack. That would break all the rules.

Besides, clearly they came from different worlds. The girl-next-door types didn't mix well with burned-out Air Force captains who'd witnessed too much of the dark side of life. He'd seen terrorists' bombs take out entire villages, had watched women and children starving in refugee camps, had heard of other atrocities he didn't want to think about.

Yep, he was going to keep his libido locked up tight. No matter if he had to take a dozen cold showers a day until this trip was over. Not just for his sake, but for hers, as well.

3

HER BODY'S INVOLUNTARY reaction to the bothersome Mr. Lockhart worried Roxie more than she cared to admit. Not only that, but she was drawn to him on an emotional level—they had a lot in common. They liked the same music and the same food. And then there was that odd feeling she got whenever he touched her, as if she'd come home after a long journey.

Ever since he'd come back from the cockpit, she felt encased in a protective bubble, as if nothing could harm her as long as he was beside her. The thought was ridiculous, but she couldn't shake it. He was so tall and strong, so commanding and reassuring.

Some corporate spy you are. Seriously, stop thinking about the dude. Keep your mind in the game or you're going to get caught.

And if that happened, Mr. Langley would have no choice but to fire her and then who would put Stacy through school? Okay, no more noticing how those pants fit so snugly to his thighs. No more imagining what his chest looked like beneath that puffy-sleeved shirt. No more sliding surreptitious glances.

Her gaze drifted over him. Wow, but he was a muscular guy. Not bodybuilder physique, but hard clean through his core. He didn't have an ounce of fat on him. His forearms were sinuous. His powerful hands bore the nicks and scars of a man who'd done manual labor. His fingers were long, his nails clean and trimmed.

His compelling profile drew her attention. He possessed

firm, no-nonsense features. Sturdy, sharp nose, angular jaw that his beard couldn't hide, lips shaped like a crossbow.

He turned and caught her studying him. His dark brown eyes, intense as an eagle's, drilled right through her. His gaze was proud and commanding, yes, but there was more. She saw compassion beneath the rough edge and a kindness he couldn't cloak. She didn't question that he would catch her if she fell; he already had.

"How does a guy like you stay single?" she asked.

Good lord, why had she said that? She couldn't have anything to do with him. He worked for Eros. She was a spy for Getaway. Not an auspicious way to start a relationship.

You're not starting a relationship. Stop thinking like that!

He arched an eyebrow and the corners of his mouth tipped up. "Pardon?"

Great, now she was going to have to repeat the question. "How come a guy like you is still single?"

Shut up! What was wrong with her? Someone should put a ball gag in her mouth.

The eyebrow shot up higher. "A guy like me?"

She could hear the chuckle in his question. "You know. Good-looking, big, strong, all protector-y?"

"Protector-y?" Amusement lit his eyes.

"I'm just saying you don't look like your typical tour guide."

"No?"

"Not so much."

"What do I look like?"

"A cop or a soldier or a fireman. Something rugged and tough."

"What about a mercenary?"

The way he said *mercenary* lifted the hairs on her forearm. "Are you a mercenary?"

"Aren't we all?" His eyes darkened and all traces of humor left his face. "In one way or another?"

Panic squeezed her lungs, snuffing out her breath. Anxiously her hand stole to her chest and she pressed her palm against her heart. Did he somehow suspect what she was up to?

Don't freak out. There's no way he can know what you're doing.

No, but if she didn't stop overreacting she was going to give herself away. "Have you ever been married?" she asked, trying to appear supercool even as she felt sweat trickle down the back of her bra.

"No."

"Ever been engaged?"

"Almost. Twice."

"What happened?"

He shrugged. "The first time we were too young, kids fresh out of high school. Luckily we both came to our senses before it was too late. The second time…"

"The second time?" she prodded. Why didn't she just pluck that romance novel out of her purse and start reading and pretend he didn't exist?

Why? Because ignoring him would be like ignoring the sun in the Sahara. He was that dominant, that powerful. And yet she couldn't help feeling he hid a vulnerable side. Had he lost someone important to him? She thought of her parents and bit down on her bottom lip.

"Let's just say that I was blindsided."

"Oh." So his ex-fiancée had cheated on him? Who would betray a guy like this? If he was her man—

Don't even go there.

But how could any woman cheat on him? In spite of the theatrical costume he wore, Dougal Lockhart was, in every sense of the word, *masculine*.

"Have you ever been engaged?" he asked.

"Me?" She shook her head. "No, no."

"You say that like the idea is preposterous."

She almost opened her mouth and told him about her parents and Stacy, but then she bit down on her tongue. She was supposed to be a spy. Spies were quiet and unobtrusive. They didn't blather. They got *other* people to talk. She shrugged.

"Not the marrying kind?" he supplied.

"Something like that."

He unbuckled his seat belt. "I've enjoyed talking to you, Roxie, but now that we're airborne and the flight has evened out, I need to schmooze with the other guests. A tour guide's work is never done."

"Oh yeah, right, sure." *Dolt, you've made him uncomfortable.*

He got out of his seat, walked back to talk to the other passengers. Instantly the sound of flirtatious laughter drifted to Roxie's ears. Who was he talking to?

Don't do it, don't look over your shoulder.

She turned to peek over the back of her seat. Dougal was leaning down, talking to two gorgeous young women a few seats behind her. He was speaking in an old English accent that should have sounded dorky, but in his deep baritone it came off sexy as sin and had Roxie wishing she'd been born in sixteenth-century England.

One of the women wore a low-cut blouse, and she was doing all she could to make sure he got a good view of her ample cleavage. The other woman was gazing at his crotch and practically drooling. These women weren't subtle. They were making it perfectly clear what they were after.

Roxie gritted her teeth.

You're jealous....

She wasn't. She was embarrassed by the flagrant way the women were throwing themselves at him. She was peeved that he seemed to be having more fun talking to them than he'd had talking to her. She was...she was...

Oh hell, she was jealous.

Why him? Why now?

It was, she decided, Eros Airlines that had pumped her up. From the buttery leather seats cushioning her fanny, to the free alcohol the flight attendants started distributing throughout the cabin, to the way Eros provocatively dressed their tour guides. She thought of the brochure in her purse, recalled the opening blurb: *Eros: where all your fantasies come true.*

The fantasy had taken hold and made her long to behave in ways she would never behave back at home. Eros had woven a spell over her, and Roxie hadn't even been aware of the spinning. Until now. Until she tried to dissect why she was feeling the way she was—lusty, jealous, greedy and intrigued.

Make notes. You need to get this down.

She reached for her purse for a pen and paper, but stopped herself. What if Dougal came back and caught her making notes? She glanced over her shoulder again. He'd moved on down the aisle, leaving twittering females in his wake. Roxie rolled her eyes.

Jealous.

Okay, so she wanted him all for herself. She wanted to kiss those commanding lips, wanted to slide her arms around that honed waist, wanted…oh, the things she wanted.

Maybe it was more than just Eros's effective marketing campaign. Maybe part of this sudden and intense desire was due to the fact she'd put her personal life on hold for the past ten years while she raised her sister. Now that Stacy was in college, Roxie finally had the opportunity to explore her sexuality.

She'd had a couple of lovers, but both relationships had ended because she wouldn't put the men above what was best for her sister. After the last relationship went sour, she'd made a promise to herself that she'd avoid romantic entanglements until Stacy was grown. Now Stacy was a college freshman, and Roxie was free to pursue a romance.

This wouldn't be a romance. This would be all about having a good time. Great sex and nothing more.

The thought of it made Roxie's ears burn. She'd never had casual sex and she had no idea how to handle something like that.

She couldn't.

She wouldn't.

Could she?

ROXIE SPENT THE REMAINDER of the flight with her nose buried in her book, doing her best to ignore Dougal's presence beside her.

They landed at Gatwick Airport around six in the evening. The minute Roxie stepped onto British soil, a fresh surge of excitement pulsed through her. Even though she worked for an airline, she'd never traveled overseas. For one thing, she hadn't wanted to be away from Stacy that long. For another there was the money issue. Although she got free flights, lodging, transfers and food didn't come cheap. Every extra bit of cash she got she stashed aside for Stacy's college tuition.

While the group waited for their luggage to be unloaded, Roxie checked her watch and subtracted the time difference. Perfect timing to call. Back at home, her sister would be in between classes, headed for lunch.

"So," Stacy answered, "how's London?"

"Right now we're at the airport. Looks pretty much like any other airport."

"Meet any cute guys yet?"

"I just got off the plane."

"Planes have been known to harbor cute guys."

"Uh-huh," Roxie said, distracted by the sight of Dougal bending over to help an older woman with a ginormous, red plaid, attack-of-the-tartans-style suitcase. The man's butt looked absolutely ferocious in leather. Absentmindedly, Roxie traced the tip of her tongue over her lips.

"Rox? You still there?"

She blinked. "Um…yeah, sure still here."

"You didn't say anything for a couple of seconds. I thought I lost you."

Resolutely she turned her back on Dougal. "Nope, you didn't lose me. I'm here. Rock solid."

"Rock-solid Roxie," Stacy echoed. "So you never did answer my question. Meet any cute guys yet?"

"I'm not here to meet guys, I—" Roxie broke off. She hadn't told her sister the real reason she was in England. She'd let her believe she was taking a vacation. Guilt nibbled at her. "I'm here for adventure."

"Guys qualify as adventures."

Roxie made a dismissive noise.

"Come on," Stacy wheedled, "when was the last time you had a date?"

"I went out with Jimmy last week."

"Listen to yourself. Jimmy is sixty-five, our second cousin, and he took you to play bingo just because he thought you needed to get out of the house. That is not a date."

"I shaved my legs for it."

"Doesn't make it a date."

"You know I decided to put my dating life on hold since things with Marcus didn't work out."

"Um…" Stacy made a disapproving sound. "I was a freshman in high school when you were going out with Marcus."

"Okay, so I haven't had much of a love life lately, I—"

"You've never had much of a love life," her sister corrected. "I've dated more guys than you and I won't turn nineteen for another three months."

"How's school?" Roxie tried changing the subject.

"Same as it was yesterday. You've only been gone for a day, Rox. Chill out. Have some fun. Find a guy. Get laid, for heaven's sake."

"Stacy!"

"Don't act so scandalized. You're young, you're hot, and you deserve to have all kinds of adventures. I thought that was the reason you picked Eros. I mean, come on, why else would a single woman sign up for an erotic fantasy vacation if she wasn't interested in indulging her erotic fantasies?"

Why indeed? She couldn't cop to being a corporate spy, so she was left with admitting that she was here for romance.

"That's why I was so happy when you told me you'd booked yourself on the Romance of Britannia tour. I thought, at last, Roxie is going to get some sex."

It felt weird having this conversation with her sister. In many ways they were more like mother and daughter than siblings. Not only was Roxie ten years her senior, she was also a lot more conservative in her outlook. Where Roxie treasured a quiet evening at home with a bowl of popcorn and a romantic comedy on DVD, her sister was the life of the party who collected friends the way some people collected shoes.

"Let's say I'm second-guessing my reasons for being here. I worry about you being home alone." That was true enough.

Stacy sighed.

"What?" An airplane took off, the noise halting their conversation for a minute. "What is it?"

"It's time you stopped using me as an excuse for putting your life on hold. I appreciate everything you've done for me, Roxie, you know that, but I can't keep being the thing that's holding you back. I feel guilty and—"

"Don't ever feel guilty," Roxie said fiercely. "Raising you has been the joy of my life."

"I'm not saying this to hurt your feelings, but you need a new joy in your life. I'm grown. I have my own friends, my own interests."

The stabbing sensation deep within her heart hit Roxie. She knew everything her sister said was true, and yet, she couldn't let go of the identity she'd taken on when their parents had been killed. Empty-nest syndrome was a bitch.

"I want you to make me a promise," Stacy said.

"What is it?"

"You have to promise first."

"I can't promise until I know what it is I'm promising to do." Roxie hardened her chin. Around her everyone was picking up their luggage and heading toward the terminal, but she barely noticed.

"Promise me if an opportunity for a vacation fling comes up, you'll grab it with both hands."

"Stace…"

"I mean it. Promise me."

"Okay, all right, on the off chance that an opportunity for mad monkey sex with a handsome stranger presents itself, I promise I'll swing through the jungle."

Stacy laughed. "You don't have to do anything that kinky, sis. Just relax and let yourself have a good time. Go with the flow. You deserve it. For ten years you've been the ultragood girl. It's okay to be a little bit bad once in a while."

"How did you get so wise?"

"I had a great teacher."

A soft, mushy sensation replaced the lost, lonely feeling in her heart. She was so proud of her baby sister. A hand settled on her shoulder. A firm, masculine hand.

"Roxie." Dougal's voice was in her ear, her name on his tongue and his scent in her nostrils.

"Who was that?" Stacy asked.

"Huh?" She played dumb.

"You're the last one left," Dougal said.

Roxie looked over at him.

He held her luggage in one hand, pointed at the tour bus waiting beyond the chain-link fence surrounding the terminal gate. "We have to go."

"It's a guy. I definitely heard a guy's voice calling your name. You sly woman, you've already met someone!"

"Listen, Stacy, I have to let you go, the tour bus is getting ready to leave and—"

"Go, Roxie, get your groove on." Stacy chanted in a silly singsong voice. "Go, Roxie, get—"

"Goodbye, little sister. Don't forget to study while I'm gone."

"You do some studying of your own. My assignment to you—get up close and personal with physical anatomy. I'm rooting for you to get lucky with your new boyfriend."

"I'm not getting lucky and he's not my boyfriend."

Stacy made clucking noises. "Chicken."

"I'll call you later." Roxie closed her cell phone to find Dougal studying her intently. Had he overhead her conversation with Stacy?

"Let's roll." He held out his arm.

An edgy, warm feeling, thrilling and unwanted, pushed through her. She wasn't going to have an affair with him just because he was good looking and she hadn't had sex in years.

"I can walk myself to the bus, thank you very much." She snatched her suitcase from his hand and scurried toward the bus. She was just about to climb on when Dougal called out to her. "Oh, Roxie."

What now? She spun on her heels, still feeling hot all over. "What is it?"

"You're getting on the wrong bus."

AFTER HE MADE SURE ROXIE got on the right bus, Dougal spoke quickly to the Eros mechanics and told them to scour the plane for problems before letting it take to the air again. Then he placed a call to Taylor, but her cell phone went to voice mail, so he left her a message.

"Taylor, Dougal," he said. "There was a glitch with the autopilot on the plane. I put your mechanics on it. Nick Peters thinks it's nothing, but I…" He paused, looked toward the waiting bus, saw Roxie in profile at a window seat near the back. In all honesty could he really say he suspected the autopilot had been tampered with? It seemed like a simple problem. If someone was making good on their threats, they'd done a lousy job of it. "I think we should wait to hear from the maintenance crew before we make any snap judgments. I'll call you later."

He closed his cell phone and slipped it into his pocket just as Roxie's eyes met his. Her gaze was steady, but he saw a flicker of something inside those cool depths.

What was it and why couldn't he shake the feeling she was up to something? She was the most unlikely of suspects.

She smiled at him then, tentative and sweet, and gave him a quick wave. And damn if he couldn't help smiling and waving back. He got a soft, achy sensation in the pit of his stomach.

Aw hell, this feeling wasn't good. Not good at all.

THE TOUR BUS TOOK THEM to the Eros resort just outside Stratford-upon-Avon. Stubborn gray clouds hung in the sky, and even inside the bus the air smelled of impending rain and city soot. The driver wore rain boots and had a black umbrella stashed under the dashboard. Dougal sat up front behind the driver and narrated the sights as they motored through the crowded streets of downtown London. Outside the window the landscape looked just like in the pictures and movies she'd seen. Imagine. She was here. England.

Roxie found herself sitting across from twin sisters, while the seat beside her remained empty. That was just fine with her.

She didn't need a traveling companion, but then she thought wistfully of Stacy and wished her sister could have joined her on this adventure.

Yeah, drag your sister along while you commit corporate espionage. What fun. Not exactly the actions of a stellar role model.

A fresh stab of conscience had Roxie worrying her bottom lip between her teeth. If Stacy's entire future didn't depend on her salary, she'd call off the whole thing.

"Hi," said the twin sitting on the outside seat. She extended her hand across the aisle to Roxie. "I'm Samantha, but everyone calls me Sam."

The other twin leaned over her sister to extend her own hand. "And I'm Jessica, but everyone calls me Jess."

She shook their hands. "Hi, Sam, hi, Jess. I'm Roxie."

"Nice to meet you, Roxie," Sam and Jess said in unison.

The twins were gorgeous, their elegant thinness a sharp contrast to Roxie's rounded curves. They possessed matching noses so perfect Roxie wondered if rhinoplasty was involved, and they had high, dramatic cheekbones enhanced by artful application of blush. They looked as if they'd stepped from the cover of a fashion magazine with their stylish bobbed blond hair and designer jeans. Beside them, she felt frumpy and out of place in her summery yellow sundress.

Sam leaned across the aisle and lowered her voice. "You are so lucky."

"Lucky?"

"You got to sit next to Shakespeare for the entire flight." Jess nodded toward Dougal.

Roxie hadn't felt lucky, she'd felt…what had she felt? *Unsettled* was the best adjective she could come up with. "I guess there's an upside to traveling alone. The tour guides take pity on you."

"So tell us," Sam breathed. "What's he like?"

Roxie shrugged. "He's just a guy."

Jess's eyes widened as if she'd said something blasphemous. "Oh, no, he's not just a guy. Look at the muscles on him. And those aren't pretty-boy, gym-induced muscles. This guy does something rugged. Rock climbing, I'm guessing."

They all three turned to look at Dougal. He was busy pointing out Big Ben.

Yes, okay, the guy was gorgeous, but jeez, people. It wasn't as if they could take him home and handcuff him to their bed or anything.

Although Jess and Sam looked as if they wouldn't mind giving it a try.

"Skiing," Sam said. "You got a guess, Roxie? Or do you already know our hunky tour guide's sport of choice?"

Roxie cocked her head and studied him—the pugilistic set to his shoulders, the broadness of his chest, and she'd already seen the scars on his knuckles. "Boxing?"

"Ooh." Jess giggled. "Astute observation. I'll bet you're right."

At that moment, Dougal turned his head and stared straight at Roxie. Awareness buzzed through her body. His eyes burned black, hot. Unable to bear the scrutiny, she fumbled his gaze.

"Mmm, mmm." Jess made a noise of appreciation. "That man is sweet."

"How come you're traveling alone?" Jess asked Roxie, after she and her sister were finished ogling Dougal. "Did a friend stand you up?"

Roxie shook her head. "I needed a private getaway."

"Ah." Sam nodded. "Busted romance."

Roxie started to correct her, but then decided to let Sam believe what she wanted to believe. She simply gave her a smile that said, "I'm putting up a brave front."

"You poor thing," Jess said. "I went through a breakup six

months ago. It's hard, but you know what? Honestly, it's the best thing that ever happened to me."

"It is." Sam nodded. "After Jess caught her fiancé doing the bedroom rumba with another woman just days before the wedding, she became a lot more assertive, and as a result of her changing attitude she got a big promotion at work."

"I stopped looking for love and just started having fun," Jess said. "Freed me up like you wouldn't believe."

"I'm envious of the easy way you approach romance." Roxie shifted her weight, did her best not to look in Dougal's direction.

"Oh, believe me," Jess said, "this is not about romance. This is about nothing but hot, hot sex."

The self-satisfied note in Jess's voice plucked a twinge of envy inside Roxie. In all honesty, she'd never been overly impressed with sex. Maybe she'd just never done it correctly.

"You've never had a casual fling?" Jess asked.

Roxie shook her head.

"Seriously, woman. It's the most liberating thing in the world. Discovering your sexual power, knowing it doesn't have to lead to anything more than it is. Glorious. Freeing."

"Really?"

"As long as you keep your heart out of the fray, and you're with the right guy, it can be mind-blowing."

"How do you keep your heart out of the fray?"

"That is a good question and it's important to prepare for it."

"I'm listening."

"First off, don't swap too many personal details about each other. No sharing intimate secrets. If you learn a lot of little details about each other, the next thing you know you start caring about them. That's not so good for a healthy casual fling," Jess advised.

"Thanks for the advice."

Sam reached over to touch Roxie on the shoulder. "Hey,

since you're all by yourself would you like to hang out with Jess and me? We'd love to have you."

The invitation shouldn't have pleased her as much as it did, and she should have thought of a graceful way to bow out. She didn't need to pal around with anyone on the tour. The more inconspicuous she made herself, the better. But she was flattered. More than that, she wanted to hang out with Jess and Sam. They seemed like a lot of fun.

"We understand if you say no," Jess hurried to add. "Since you've caught the attention of our tour guide. He hasn't stopped looking at you this entire ride. You might want to spend your time hanging out with him."

Roxie didn't dare turn her head to meet his stare. "I'm not interested in a romance."

"Who said anything about a romance?" Jess made a purring noise. "I'd just love to have a fling with him. If you're really not interested that is."

Roxie couldn't bring herself to say that she wasn't interested. There was that damned jealousy again. Illogical and annoying.

"Anyway," Sam said, "we'll save a place for you at dinner, unless Mr. Handsome Man over there sweeps you off your feet."

All in all, Roxie didn't have many friends. Of course Stacy was her best friend. There was Magda at work, and Mrs. Kingsly who lived across the street, and Susan, the checker at the supermarket. But they were all over thirty-five and married with children. She didn't really have anyone her own age she could relate to.

You can't hang out with them. You're here under false pretenses. Tell them you appreciate the offer, but you have other plans. Tell them you're hoping for a romance and you're worried guys will be less likely to approach women in a group than on their own.

Tell them…

She opened her mouth to use one of her excuses, but instead she spoke from her heart. "Sure, I'd love to hang out with you guys. Thanks for asking."

4

THE EROS RESORT WAS a hedonist's wet dream.

From the outside the place was picturesque. The main building was a replica of a sixteenth-century castle perched on a sloping green hill overlooking the river Avon, complete with its own moat. Inside the castle grounds, snug little thatch cottages were lumped like gray-green turtles along a unifying cobblestone path. The moment Roxie stepped off the bus in the thickening drizzle, she was hit with the acute sensation that her world had just cracked wide-open and she'd stepped into a fairy tale.

She tried not to stare openmouthed, but it was a bit difficult when they were met at the door by a cadre of bellmen all dressed in the same romantic sixteenth-century style as Dougal and speaking in the tongue of that time. They flirted and winked. Clearly it was their intention to make the guests feel both lusty and welcome.

"Let me take that for you, milady." A dashing bellboy, looking for all the world like Romeo Montague from Shakespeare's most famous play, bowed and relieved Roxie of her suitcase.

Jess and Sam tittered as similarly outfitted bellmen took their luggage.

The five-star rated resort's lobby was a sight to behold. It looked both old world and elegant and deadly romantic with huge vases of fresh-cut roses, Stargazer lilies and gladiola resting on highly polished antique tables. The air was scented with their sweet fragrance. The sofas and chairs placed strategically throughout the cavernous lobby were upholstered in rich matching fabrics of cranberry and gold. In the middle of the lobby was a grand fireplace made of gray lintels carved with quatrefoils and spanned by a four-centered arch with molded decorations and a frieze topping the lintels. Over the mantel hung a stately coat of arms.

Stenciled on the walls in gilded script lettering outlined in black were famous quotes about love. Her gaze traveled around the room as she read the slogans.

Naughty, naughty. Roxie pressed her fingers against her mouth, suppressing a grin. Just then a pretty female assistant dressed in a gauzy floor-length gown and a crown of braided flowers wandered over to distribute small flutes of complimentary ice wine to the thirsty travelers queuing up at the registration desk.

Roxie sipped her drink. She was delighted to discover it tasted like golden honey, sweet and thick and pure. She didn't imbibe often, and just a couple of swallows produced a warm glow that drew her deeper into the magical atmosphere. Porter Langley had no idea what he was getting into if he set his cap at competing with Taylor Corben's lavish destination resorts.

While they were waiting their turn to check in, an older woman, dressed in the same Tudor style as the young assistant, passed out a form printed on white card stock. "Hi, my name is Lucy Kenyon and I'm the entertainment director. To help tailor this experience to meet your needs, I'd appreciate it if you'd fill out this questionnaire and leave it with me."

Roxie took the form and read through the short list of questions. Most of them were centered on her personal likes and dislikes. She answered as best she could, but paused when she got to the end.

"What are your hobbies, special skills or talents that you still love but haven't had time for lately?" Jess read the last line on her card out loud just as Roxie poised her pen to answer it.

The question hit home. It had been so long since she'd gotten to do the things she'd given up after her parents' tragic car accident. Becoming a surrogate parent at eighteen had caused her to grow up quickly. She felt a tug of emotion in her belly, a sadness mixed with yearning for everything she'd lost. She didn't regret giving up leisurely pursuits for Stacy, but she did miss them, and she hadn't really realized it until now.

"Oh gosh," Sam said. "I guess we're spoiled. We pretty much do everything we love."

"What about you, Roxie?" Jess asked. "What are you putting down?"

Roxie doodled on the edge of the form, remembering how she used to enjoy acting. She'd even toyed with the idea of majoring in drama when she went to college.

Except she'd never gotten to college.

"I used to enjoying acting," she admitted.

Sam nudged Jess. "You used to be able to whistle 'Battle Hymn of the Republic.' That's a special skill."

Jess rolled her eyes. "It's not one I want to revisit. Anything else you used to like to do, but don't get to do now, Roxie?"

"Fencing."

Sam blinked. "You like putting up fences?"

"No, dork," Jess told her twin. "You know, *en garde.*" She illustrated with a badly executed fencing pose. "Like Zorro."

"Ah, that kind of fencing." Sam nodded.

"My father qualified for the Olympic fencing team when he was twenty," Roxie shared with her new friends. "But my mother had just found out she was pregnant with me and he chose not to go."

"That's so sweet and romantic," Sam said.

"Fencing was one activity we did together, just he and I."

And she hadn't picked up a foil since his death. Roxie blinked, swallowed past the lump in her throat and wrote down acting and fencing in answer to the final question.

"Oh, I know," Jess said. "We used to go with Dad on stake-outs. Let's put down sleuthing."

"Your father was a cop?" Roxie asked.

"P.I.," Sam explained and frowned at her twin. "Sleuthing isn't going to come in handy around here."

"How do you know they're not going to have one of those mystery theater events? We'd kick ass."

"I'll take those, thanks." Lucy Kenyon smiled and plucked the forms from Roxie, Jess and Sam. "And when you're finished with registration, please feel free to visit the costume room. Many of our guests enjoy dressing up for the events."

"You have a costume room?" Roxie asked. She loved role-playing.

"We do." Lucy indicated an area at the back of the lobby before she turned to greet new arrivals.

"Wow." Jess craned her neck upward. "Get a load of that ceiling."

Roxie glanced up and gulped. While the lobby was pure class, the ceiling was pure erotica, albeit tastefully executed. Near-naked men and women frolicked overhead in what could be best described as an orgy about to happen. Lots of succulent fruit was involved in the suggestive tableau—hard yellow-green bananas, plump plums, curvy pears, ripe red strawberries, brilliantly orange kumquats. She could almost taste the sinful fruit salad.

Embarrassed, she jerked her gaze away from the sight and stepped back only to crash into someone behind her.

A masculine hand went to her elbow. "Steady."

She spun around, found herself face-to-face with Dougal, her cheeks scalding hot. "Um…I…er…"

Immediately her gaze was drawn to his enigmatic eyes. Did the man have any idea how compellingly sexy he looked in the white loose-sleeved silk shirt that floated over his broad masculine shoulders and those snug-fitting leather breeches that enhanced even more fascinating parts of his anatomy? Roxie shook her head, determined to empty her mind of such inappropriate thoughts.

He took a step closer and she caught a whiff of his scent— leather, sandalwood soap and man. She couldn't help noticing the softness of his windblown hair. She suppressed the disconcerting urge to reach out and tame the unruly strands with her fingers just to see if it was as soft as it looked.

"It is a bit overwhelming at first glance." His eyes twinkled.

"Huh?"

"The castle, the lobby, the ceiling."

"Um, yeah," she mumbled, not knowing what else to say, not sure she could or should say anything more. For one vivid flash of her imagination she'd pictured herself and Dougal joining the madcap couples on the ceiling, and that thought escalated the blistering of her cheeks. The fantasy overloaded her senses. Her muscles tensed. Her heart beat faster. It was in that moment she realized the stereo system was very quietly, almost subliminally, playing a seductive sound track of twin heartbeats beneath the lyrical flute music.

Looking into Dougal's eyes, hearing the steady strum-strum-strumming sound, smelling flowers, tasting fruit and ice wine, feeling his fingers at her elbow sent her emotions into tumult.

The primal music became an exclamation mark, underscoring her befuddlement, igniting her feminine passion. Her desire tasted of hot musk. The drumming altered with the changes inside her, growing deeper, more intricate and multifaceted. She felt this sudden and unexpected need everywhere—in her toes, in the pads of her fingertips, in the muscles of her buttocks. She'd never experienced anything like it and the air left her lungs on one expanded sigh.

He was standing way too near her, but she didn't know how to tell him to back off. If he were to dip his head down to say something to her, his lips would be kissably close. She retreated a step, her thoughts a chaotic tumble of craziness.

"Next," called the clerk behind the check-in desk.

"You're up."

Dazed, Roxie blinked at him. "What?"

Dougal nodded toward the desk. "You're next."

"Oh, right."

The spell was shattered. Dougal smiled and then turned and walked away.

AN HOUR LATER, DOUGAL entered the ballroom for the eight o'clock dinner seating. It bothered him that he hadn't been able to stop thinking about Roxie. What was it about her that had so slipped underneath his skin? He thought about her scent, delicate and sweet. Some kind of flower. Honeysuckle? Or maybe those white flowers that grew on those thick waxy-leaved trees in the South.

The way she looked at him in the lobby, wide-eyed and blushing, caused his gut to clench and his cock to harden. This was crazy. He was crazy. He was on assignment. He had to get his head in the game.

You're just falling victim to the Eros experience—the subliminal music, the suggestive paintings, the flowers, the candlelit sconces lining the hallways. Snap out of it.

As a tour guide, Dougal was expected to mingle with the guests, and he found himself seated at a table with two busty women who sat on either side of him and kept stroking his forearms. He felt like a piece of hamburger, but he endured it for the job, his gaze going around the room, looking for anything or anyone suspicious.

And then his eyes lighted on Roxie. She was seated at a table with the twin sisters she'd sat next to on the bus, looking up at one of the waiters, a man dressed in a troubadour costume. She was asking questions about the menu. The man leaned over, his shoulder brushing against Roxie's, his stare traveling straight down the cleavage of her dress.

Dougal suppressed an overwhelming urge to vault over the table and snap the man's neck like a twig. The impulse was so strong that he sucked in a whistle of air. *Whoa!* What was this all about?

Roxie smiled and handed her menu to the waiter, who went on to the next guest.

Dougal unclenched his jaw, said something to the woman on his right while the woman on his left ran her fingers up his arm. This kind of attention made him uncomfortable. He glanced at Roxie again.

She looked like dessert in that flowing period-piece costume and she had her sleek black hair pinned up off her shoulders, making her look even younger and sweeter. No woman her age could be that innocent. Her ingenuousness heightened his mistrust, at the same time his gut told him, *She's a keeper.*

This feeling unnerved him and that was reason enough to raise his guard, but it was more than that. It was the damned sexual attraction that scared him most. There was something so disarmingly appealing about this woman and being disarmed was not a position he ever wanted to be in again.

Their eyes met—*wham.*

He smiled, nodded.

She smiled back.

They held each other's gazes for too long, and then they both veered away at the same moment like two back alley drag racers with not enough bravado to see their game of chicken play out to a conclusion.

A fresh surge of blood rushed his groin. Something inside Dougal stirred and it wasn't just his dick. Something he really didn't want to identify. He took a swig from the mug of beer in front of him.

A hand on his shoulder caused him to jump. He yanked his head around and saw the recreational events director, Lucy Kenyon, standing beside him. Lucy was a lithe brunette in her early forties. He'd checked her credentials as he had all of Taylor's employees. She was recently divorced, her kids grown, and she was finally experiencing her lifelong dream of living in England. Like the rest of the staff, she was dressed in a costume representative of the Tudor era. "We're ready to start the entertainment portion of the evening, Dougal."

He put down his napkin, scooted back his chair and followed Lucy to the stage, feeling like a condemned man on his way to the gallows. This was the part of the assignment he dreaded. Dougal was loath to admit it, even to himself, but he was nervous. They'd practiced the skit, but this was the first time he'd performed in front of a live audience and his childhood issues with stage fright rumbled to life. Suddenly he was eight years old again, playing an onion in a play about the four food groups.

The ugly memory came rushing back as he climbed the steps of the stage behind the red velvet curtain. Eight years old and he'd barely been able to see through the eyeholes in the rotund, papier-mâché onion. It had smelled like paste and plaster and body odor from the previous kid who'd worn it.

Before the play, Dougal's mother had given him ginger ale to calm his stomach. The bubbly taste was sparkly sharp on his tongue, but he hadn't been the least bit calmed. Inside the dank, mushroomlike costume, he could barely hear what the narrator at the microphone had been telling the audience, but he could hear their laughter. His palms had been sweaty, his heart knotted tight in his chest, his knees wobbled as the spotlight had fallen on him and he'd looked out into the sea of faces.

They were all laughing and staring at him, just waiting for him to mess up.

And mess up he had.

When it was his turn to extol the benefits of five servings of fruits and vegetables a day, he'd opened his mouth and puked all over his sneakers. He'd had an aversion to onions ever since.

Ah, good times. Good times.

Why had he agreed to Taylor's insane plans?

For the money.

Oh yeah, there was that. Starting a private air marshal enterprise took a lot of time and money. A client like Taylor would cinch his reputation. It was time to face the horror of his oniony past and put it to rest once and for all.

"Find one person to focus on," Lucy whispered, somehow sensing his stage fright. Was he that transparent? "Perform only for that one person and it will calm the butterflies."

Right. Gotcha. He'd give it a try.

The sketch they were set to perform was a riff on the legend that Shakespeare left his second-best bed to his wife, Anne Hathaway. Anne had been eight years older than her famous husband. For entertainment purposes, Lucy was laughingly playing Anne as a sixteenth-century cougar. Dougal had the part of the Bard. The skit wasn't remotely historically correct, but rather it was designed as a bit of raunchy humor to kick off the Romance of Britannia two-week tour and set the tone for the adventure the guests were embarking upon.

At the microphone stood the emcee, a lean, long-haired young man dressed like a court jester. He welcomed the guests and then began setting up the scenario for the spoof.

Dougal took a deep breath. *Come on, you've been in charge of guarding fighter jets. You can handle this goofy piece of fluff with your eyes closed.* Closing his eyes? Was that an option? Right now dental surgery sounded like a more appealing alternative.

The curtain parted. The audience applauded. His stomach pitched.

In the center of the stage sat a four-poster king-size bed decked out with a baroque crimson comforter and matching pillows. It looked like whorehouse bedding. Lucy recited her line, and then she shot a glance at Dougal.

His brain froze. He couldn't think. He opened his mouth but no words came out.

Find one person to focus on.

He didn't plan it. How could he plan it when he couldn't think? His gaze swung through the audience and lighted on Roxie.

Perform only for her.

Roxie held Dougal's stare. To his surprise, the words that had been locked inside his head suddenly fell glibly from his lips. "Forsooth, madam, pray what shall I leave thee when I die? Perhaps my second-best bed?"

Lucy's advice had worked. Who knew it would be so simple?

"And which of these trollops shall inherit this, your finest bed?" Lucy waved at the bed and sneered. Then she comically narrowed her eyes and glanced out over the crowd as if they were her rivals for Shakespeare's affections.

"It shall be your choice," Dougal replied, his attention still locked on Roxie. "Select the lass with whom I will be sharing my bed."

"Three in a bed seems a bit crowded, husband," Lucy replied saucily. "Perhaps she and I will kick you out."

That line caused a titter to run through the crowd.

"Or perhaps," Lucy went on, "I shall select a lad to join us."

"Only a lass will do, woman." Dougal recited his lines.

"Pick her and pick her quick or I won't even leave you my second-best bed."

"As you wish." Lucy started down the steps to select someone from the audience to bring up onstage and a dozen hands shot up to volunteer.

"Pick me, pick me," someone called out.

"I'd love to spend time in Shakespeare's bed," said someone else.

"I'll whisper dirty limericks in his ear," hollered the audacious redhead who'd made yummm-o noises at Dougal on the airplane.

Lucy threaded her way through the tables, ignoring all the women who were straining to volunteer. She continued to speak her lines as she and Dougal bantered back and forth.

She stopped at Roxie's table.

And that's when Dougal realized Lucy was going to bring her up onstage.

5

"HI," ANNE HATHAWAY SAID.

Roxie recognized her as Lucy Kenyon, the woman who'd passed out the questionnaires in the lobby when they'd first arrived. She gulped and realized everyone at the table was watching her. Who was she kidding? Everyone in the *room* was watching her, even Dougal. For crying out loud, there was a spotlight on her. "Um…hi."

Lucy leaned in closer. "I saw on our survey that you enjoy acting."

"Yes," she replied, not knowing what else to say.

"Would you like to have some fun?"

They were magic words. Roxie knew that she should say no, but in that moment, all the joy of being onstage rushed through her. She recalled the fun she used to have performing at her parents' dinner theater, and remembered her role as the lead in her high school's production of *Romeo and Juliet*. In the school's history, no freshman had ever been given the lead role before her.

Roxie couldn't help smiling even as she said, "I don't know the lines."

"That's what we want, off-the-cuff improv. Come on," Lucy coaxed. "It'll be fun."

"Go on." Sam nudged her.

"You get to be onstage with Shakespeare," Jess pointed out. "Go for it, woman."

Roxie hesitated, but only for a moment. The ham in her took over and she nodded.

"Wonderful." Lucy held out her hand to Roxie and led her to the stage.

Her heart was pounding, but the minute she was facing the audience, exuberance embraced her. It had been so long since she'd done something solely for herself and she felt liberated.

"Lie down on this bed, fair maiden," Anne instructed, patting the mattress with a naughty gleam in her eyes. "And pray tell us your impression of my husband's best bed."

Giddily Roxie slid onto the bed and lay back against the pillows. The silky material of the pink, flower-print Renaissance frock she'd picked out from the costume room rubbed erotically against her skin. The tight bodice pulled across her nipples, causing them to bead beneath her camisole. Belatedly she realized she should have worn a bra instead.

"Wife," Shakespeare aka Dougal said, "you have chosen a comely lass."

"I did so for the benefit of my eyes, sir, not thine own." Anne gave Roxie a seductive look.

"However, wife, I am enjoying your feast." Dougal was looking at Roxie as if she were dipped in chocolate. He angled his head, licked his lips.

The crowd chuckled.

"So, maiden—" Anne swept across the stage "—what is thy opinion of the master's bed?"

Relishing her role, Roxie bounced up and down. The bedsprings creaked loudly. "'Tis a bit loud, milady. Might it wake the children?"

"Ah," said Dougal. "Shouldn't children learn that squeaky bedsprings are simply a part of grown-up life?"

"It's a bit too hard, as well," Roxie observed, flopping about on the mattress for effect.

"I told him it was too hard." Anne looked pointedly at Shakespeare's crotch, inducing catcalls from the audience.

Shakespeare and Anne bickered back and forth over the prone Roxie, each line of dialogue filled with ribald statements and sexy innuendo. Roxie rolled her eyes and heaved exaggerated sighs over their squabbling. "Married couples," she said as an aside to the audience.

The more she hammed it up, the louder the laughter grew. She was aware of—and exalting in—the fact that she was stealing the show.

Anne Hathaway said something to Shakespeare, but he didn't answer. A momentary silence fell over the crowd. Roxie turned her head to see Dougal staring at her as if they were the only two people in the room.

The expression on his face stole her breath. Her pulse skittered, and she felt twin dots of heat rise to her cheeks. She pursed her lips and crossed her arms chastely over her chest. It was as if he'd stripped her stark naked with his inscrutable gaze.

Lucy repeated her line, nudging him in the side with her elbow.

"Um…er…" Dougal sputtered.

"I can see the fetching vixen has stolen your tongue, husband," Anne said.

"No vixen, she," Dougal said, finally finding his voice. "But she is the very muse that moves my soul."

As Dougal stared into her eyes, Roxie felt as if the words were suddenly, oddly, illogically true. Her body grew heavy with sexual awareness and she felt herself go slick between her thighs. She gulped, disoriented.

Shake it off. What are you doing?

A corporate spy should fly under the radar. Getting up onstage was not the way to keep a low profile. But while her professional side berated her for this dumb move, her personal side was secretly reveling, having fun, doing the unexpected.

That is, until Dougal walked across the stage and plunked down on the bed, never breaking eye contact with her. He was beside her again as if he belonged there, turning her on.

She'd had daydreams like this, midnight reveries. Imaging herself a throwback to the Renaissance era. Such a romantic epoch filled with great art and music and the concept of chivalry. Dougal was the embodiment of her sexual fantasies.

Oh, dear. She couldn't tear her gaze off him. What to do? What to do? And here she'd thought falling into his lap on the plane had been erotic. But *this* was a hundred times more intense. They were side by side.

On a mattress.

Lying mere inches apart.

With a roomful of people watching their every move.

She could feel the power of his muscular body underneath his costume. She appreciated the natural mahogany highlights in his neatly trimmed beard. Surely no man in history had ever looked so manly in snug, black leather pants, a billowy white poet's shirt and knee-length black boots.

Eat your heart out, William Shakespeare.

The shadow falling over his face lent his expression a darkly dangerous air that was so damned sexy the hairs on her forearm lifted in response. One close-up glance at his angular mouth and all she could think about was kissing him. Her breathing quickened and her heart tripped over itself.

The collective laughed in response to something Anne Hathaway had said as she tromped in mock fury away from the bed, reminding Roxie where she was. Why had she agreed to come up onstage? Ego? The opportunity to live out her childhood fantasy of becoming an actress? To recapture her past? A chance to be near Dougal again?

Roxie feared the third option was the most accurate. What

was it about the man that made her want to live out a very X-rated *adult* fantasy?

"Forsooth," Anne called out to the audience, hand clasped to her bosom. "You are all my witnesses. Look upon my husband and see how he stares at the temptress. Has she not cast such a spell on him that he is left both speechless and brainless?"

Dougal looked stunned, as if he, too, had forgotten where he was and what he was supposed to be doing. Immediately he leaped from the bed, hair tousled and shirt askew. He placed a hand at the nape of his neck and stared down at Roxie, then quickly shifted his attention to Lucy.

"You are right, wife, I have been bewitched," he exclaimed.

"Trollop." Anne pointed an accusing finger at Roxie. "You have stolen the bed that should have been rightfully mine."

Okay. This wasn't fair. Roxie didn't have any lines and she had no way to know what was expected of her.

Improvise.

"Perhaps, milady," Roxie dared, going up on her knees in the middle of the bed, "if you had but satisfied your husband in this very bed, then he would not seek solace within my arms."

Both Shakespeare and his wife turned to stare at her, while the audience hooted with glee.

Roxie grinned at Dougal.

He grinned back, clearly enjoy her improvisational skills. "She has a point, good wife."

Anne looked a bit confused as what to say next. Roxie's input had knocked the skit off its trajectory. "All I want," Anne said at last, "is what's rightfully mine."

"Your husband?" Dougal said, stepping across the stage toward Anne with his arms outstretched.

"My bed," Anne cried, made a comical face and hopped onto the mattress beside Roxie.

The crowd dissolved into guffaws.

Dougal shrugged, raised his palms to the audience as if to say, "Easy come, easy go," and then held his hand out to Roxie. "Take the bed, wife, and I will take my muse."

Roxie didn't take his hand.

Dougal repeated his line, wriggled his eyebrows at her and added, "Come along, Muse."

Swept away by the thrill of performance, feeling decidedly impish, Roxie collapsed against the pillows. "My lord," she said. "This mattress is too desirable to leave."

"I thought it was too hard."

"Perhaps I was hasty in my judgment. For now it feels just right."

"Muse!" he bellowed and strode toward the bed, hand still outstretched. "Come here at once."

Excitement welled up, pushed against Roxie's chest, sent tingles shooting out through her nerve endings.

"Go get her, Shakespeare," a woman in the crowd yelled out.

"Shoot for the ménage à trois, Willie," countered a man.

Anne flashed a suggestive look at the audience that said she was intrigued by the prospect.

Shakespeare stopped, pivoted on his heel and peered out at the gathered guests. "Some men are foolish enough to think they can handle more than one woman at a time. I, however, am smart enough to know it's best to be a one-muse man."

"What about me?" Anne lamented.

"You, milady, have not been so much muse as nag," Shakespeare answered.

That brought fresh laughter.

Shakespeare turned his attention back to Roxie. "Now, Muse, come along, I have a sonnet in want of being written."

"What?" Roxie crossed her arms over her chest. "I do all the work and you get all the credit? The deal does not sound so fetching to me. How about this? I write my own sonnet."

"He gets bossy like this," Anne interjected. "Is his best bed really worth putting up with his high-handedness?"

"I need you, Muse." Dougal's words sounded so heartfelt that Roxie's pulse quickened. He extended his hand. "Pray, do not abandon me."

"He'll abandon *you*," Anne warned, studying her nails with a nonchalant expression. "Next thing you know, it'll be a younger, prettier muse booting you out of bed."

"Don't listen to her," he said. "She's jealous."

Just like that, Roxie's improvisational skills evaporated. She whipped her head around to look at Anne, searching for a clue as to what to say next. Anne shrugged. Her expression said, *You're on your own.* Roxie was suddenly aware that every eye in the ballroom was on her, waiting to see what she'd do next. The urge to flee smacked her hard.

"Come." Dougal reached out; his hand barely grazed her knuckles and yet she felt blindsided.

Helpless to deny him, she rested her palm in his hand and he tugged her to her feet. His eyes hooked on hers, and she could not look away no matter how much she might desire to do so. Then, in his spine-tingling, baritone voice, Dougal began to recite a Shakespearean sonnet.

She knew the verse. She'd been forced to memorize it as part of a high school English assignment. Sonnet number twenty-one: "So is it not with me as with that Muse."

Kismet.

Dougal said a line, and then Roxie jumped in with the next one. His eyes lit up. They went back and forth with perfect timing as if they'd practiced this duet for weeks. He was holding her hands and they were staring deeply into each other's eyes and it was pure magic. This shared verbal intermingling was simply the most erotic thing she'd ever done with her clothes on.

The audience went wild for it.

"Woot!" she heard Jess holler. "Rock on, Roxie."

"Shake it, Willie!" Sam shouted.

Roxie recited the last line in a throaty whisper.

Dougal's jaw tightened. His chest muscles—readily visible through the deep V of the undone buttons on his shirt—flexed. The pulse at the hollow of his throat strengthened, slowed. He drew in a deep breath and slowly exhaled it as if by controlling his breathing he could control other responses.

Her body reacted to his physical clues. A warm gush of awareness oozed through her skin already heated by the overhead spotlights. She hadn't realized it until now, but the entire time they'd been reciting the sonnet, they'd been inching closer and closer to each other. Mostly unconscious of what she was doing, Roxie ran her tongue over her lips, tasting the poetic beauty of the sonnet.

His fingers were interlaced with hers. When had that happened? The tips of his leather boots were touching her sandals. Barely an inch of space existed between them. Their hip bones were almost touching, his chest so close she fancied she could hear his beating heart, and then realized it was her own heart she heard pounding with alarming power.

He glanced down. Her gaze followed his and she saw the tightness across the front fly of his pants.

This was insanity. They were total strangers. Not to mention that they were onstage in front of dozens of people with spotlights trained on them. Yet all Roxie could think about was throwing her arms around Dougal's neck to see if his mouth tasted as good as it looked.

Before she had a chance to do something rash, though, he took the reins. He slid an arm around her waist and pulled her tightly against him. She saw his eyes darken with desire, and she wondered if her own were undergoing the same changes.

The next thing she knew, they were kissing.

DOUGAL HAD FOUND HIMSELF lost in a fairy tale—the audience disappeared, Anne vanished, the spotlight no longer existed, the stage faded away. The only thing left in his world was *her.*

It was hard to say who made the first move. It was simultaneous really. When Roxie pulled his head down to meet her lips, Dougal breathed in the taste of her and tightened his grip around her waist. He'd been aching to kiss her from the moment he'd seen her in the plane, and damn if he didn't just let it happen.

She tasted as good as she looked. Better even. Her flavor was fresh and lemony and sensational. Initially, kissing her made him think of his mother's kitchen—warm and safe and comfortable. But underneath that soft comfort roused a stronger, more primal instinct.

Lust. Hot and heavy and intense.

And in spite of the wide-eyed innocent image she projected, what she was doing to him with her mouth was anything but innocent. He could get seriously addicted to this.

Dougal swallowed back a groan of pleasure at the feel of her thigh against his. She curled her fingers into his scalp, pressed her body into him, crushing her soft breasts against the silky Shakespeare shirt. His entire body caught fire. Without meaning to do so, he raised his hand to cup her buttocks.

She gasped.

It was only then he realized he'd closed his eyes, gotten washed away on a dream. Startled by the thought, his eyes flew open. Roxie's eyes were open, as well, and she was looking at him with a mixture of curiosity, amazement, excitement and mortification.

Dougal pulled his lips away.

She stared at him with those incredible blue eyes, her pupils dark and wide. She touched the tip of her tongue to her upper lip as if still thirsty for his taste.

He felt it, too, this thirst.

The audience members were on their feet, clapping wildly. "Bravo!"

"Encore."

"Make use of that bed!"

Roxie blushed, and Dougal recognized that everyone thought the kiss was part of the skit. She turned toward the crowd and took a bow.

Suddenly Dougal was confused. Had she been playing a part? Had Roxie been a plant in the audience? She'd been so quick on her feet with the ad libs. Perhaps it hadn't been improv after all. What was going on? Was Lucy in on this?

"You were great," he said.

She beamed. "Thank you. Not too shabby yourself."

He couldn't tear his gaze off her, and then overhead, he heard an ominous creaking noise.

"Look out!" someone in the audience shouted.

Dougal glanced up just in time to see that a spotlight had come loose from its mounting. It dangled precariously by an electrical cord, swaying directly over their heads.

The crowd gasped.

Dougal reacted out of pure instinct, pushing Roxie aside just as the heavy spotlight came crashing to the stage.

6

ROXIE LAY SPRAWLED on the floor, Dougal's big body pressed down on hers, his chest squashing her breasts, his warm breath heating her cheek. His pelvis was flush against hers, and he'd brought his arms up around her head to protect her.

Her heart thundered—from danger, from fear, from this man's proximity. Her ears rang. Her head spun. Her womb tightened reflexively. Disoriented both by lack of oxygen and his compelling, masculine scent, she simply stared up into his mesmerizing dark eyes.

What had just happened?

Why had Dougal knocked her to the stage?

She was vaguely aware of people converging on them, talking, letting out exclamations of surprise and asking questions, but all her focus was on him.

"Roxie," he whispered huskily, "are you okay?"

Lines of concern etched his forehead, pulled his angular mouth downward. Bits of broken glass glinted in his hair, clung to his beard. She frowned, still trying to piece together what had happened, still trying to make sense of the raging sexual awareness heightening her senses.

He rolled off her then, and air rushed into her lungs. He reached down to help her up. Once on her feet, Roxie's gaze shifted from Dougal to the twisted metal and shattered glass that was once the overhead spotlight. Reality hit her all at once.

"We could have been…ki-killed," she stammered.

"We weren't."

"You saved my life."

"Saved mine, too." He grinned humbly and shook his head to dislodge the glass. The simple action shouldn't have been sensual, but the way he raked his fingers through the chocolaty strands, mussing it with his thick fingers, captivated her.

And the way his shirt gaped open, revealing his honed chest muscles and a sprinkling of dark chest hairs, sent a sharp spike of pure physical longing jettisoning straight to her sex.

Roxie blinked. What was wrong with her? She'd almost been obliterated by a falling spotlight and all she could think about was how utterly delicious Dougal looked. She didn't have much time to consider her question because security and maintenance personnel appeared to assess the situation, while Lucy Kenyon and other staff members rounded up the guests and ushered them out of the dining room.

"You're trembling," Dougal said.

"Am I?" Surprised, Roxie realized her hands were quivering.

"Shock," he said. "Spent adrenaline."

Ah, maybe that could explain her inappropriately sexual thoughts. Chemistry, a hormonal response to stress.

"Come on," he said. "I'll walk you back to your cottage."

The moonlit walk across the cobblestone path deepened the odd spell she seemed to be under. The air was damp but sweet with the smell of springtime flowers, and a tinkling of flute music flowed through speakers placed strategically about the grounds. Dougal held her hand the entire way, only letting go when they reached the bungalow where she was staying.

"Here we are," he said.

"Here we are," she echoed.

"That was fun tonight," he said. "The skit I mean, not almost getting beaned by the spotlight."

"That was pretty amazing, how we got a rhythm going."

"Like great sex."

Why had he said that? Now all she could think was sex, sex, sex. Inhaling sharply, she met his gaze and got totally sucked in by those fascinating brown orbs. As she watched, his mercurial eyes changed from sweet milk chocolate to pure smoldering cocoa, the color a tantalizing complement to his ebony lashes and rich, dark brows.

His full lips quirked up at the corners as he shot her what she was quickly starting to recognize as a "come sin" grin. He might appear cool and controlled, but beneath that detached exterior she detected a current of something hot and taut and wild. The man was pure energy, raw and alive.

She was seriously screwed. With a sinking sensation she realized just how much she wanted him to kiss her.

He stood there, his hand at her waist, wearing the sexiest damn smile she had ever seen. How easy it would be to drag him into her cottage and make love to him. How easy and yet how utterly scary. She shouldn't. She couldn't. She wouldn't.

Kiss me, kiss me, kiss me.

Dougal moistened his mouth.

Roxie flicked out the tip of her tongue to wet her own lips.

He lowered his head.

Her heart jumped into her throat. His face was so close she could almost feel the brush of his beard against her cheek. *Kiss me, kiss me, kiss me.*

He pressed his mouth to her ear. She closed her eyes and leaned into him. Her body tensed…waiting, wanting, willing.

Dougal sucked in an audible breath. She tipped up her head. The look on his face was so feral, so hungry, as if it was all he could do to control his sexual urges. Her hands started quivering all over again. Did she really hold that much sexual power over him?

"Shakespeare," she whispered.

"Muse," he said, playing into her fantasy.

She wrapped her arms around his neck, and he pulled her close, nestling her into the curve of his body. She felt the determined poke of his penis through his leather breeches, but he made no move to take things further. He was long, thick and hard, no secrets on that score. She thought of them both naked, imagined him inside her, filling her up. They stood on the stoop, swaying together in the breeze.

She tried to deny the desire pushing up through her, closed her eyes and forced herself to concentrate on something other than the need knotting her entire body, but it was impossible.

They breathed in tandem, but Dougal did not make a move on her.

What in the hell was wrong with the man? How was he staying so controlled? And the more restraint he showed, the more desperately she wanted him.

She thought about all she'd missed out on in life. Fun, a good time, casual dating, casual sex. Suddenly she wanted to experience it all. Now. With Dougal. She was in England, at a hot, sexy, romantic resort. There was nothing stopping her from just enjoying good sex for good sex's sake.

Do it. Sleep with this man. You know you want to. It doesn't have to mean happily ever after, just happily right now.

She felt a racy sense of exuberance, of glorious feminine power. Like a moth on the wind, carried by the swell of pheromones, she let herself be swept away and did something she'd never done before.

She pulled out her best acting skills, pretending to be a saucy serving wench from the sixteenth century.

Roxie kissed him.

DOUGAL SHOULD HAVE BROKEN the kiss, pushed her away, fought his Neanderthal impulses, which were urging him to kick down the door and drag her into the cottage and have his way with her. He'd come here to make sure she was okay and he was trying to sort out in his mind whether the falling spot-light had been accidental or intentional.

But the fact that she—little Miss Innocence—had kissed him destroyed his capacity to think straight.

He took the kiss to a whole new level, dragged her tight against him, plundering her mouth with his, drinking her in. His head spun, his heart pounded. Some security expert he was turning out to be. He didn't even remember where he was, much less why he was here. All he knew was that he had to have more of Roxie.

His hand had a mind of its own, slipping down to cup her tight, round bottom. His cock strained against his fly. Flexing, he curled his fingers into the soft, willing flesh of her buttocks. He heard her quick intake of breath, and he couldn't believe what he was doing, squeezing her so possessively.

You're out of line.

But he couldn't stop kissing her or touching her. She was even tastier than in his fantasies. Her mouth was hot and moist and so was his. He kneaded her bottom and she trembled against him.

The air vibrated between them. The erotic promise buried in their kiss made him shudder. The push of her rose-petal lips dis-oriented him. His tongue traced the form and curve of her mouth. Supped from the delightful swell of her lower lip, the sculpted bow of the upper, explored the textured velvet of her mouth.

His need for her went beyond all reason. He'd never felt anything like this. He should escape while he could, but then she pulled her lips from his and whispered, "Would thee like to come inside, Shakespeare?"

No, no, say no.

But his stupid tongue did not obey. She was pulling him

headlong into her fantasy. What he said was, "Forsooth, there is nothing I would enjoy more, Mistress Muse."

She unlocked the door, flicked on the light, drew him inside the room with her. The door snapped closed behind them.

Blood pumped through his veins at a crazy rhythm. She tipped her head coyly, smiled at him. The shy girl was back, all sweet and demure. Which one was the real Roxie? The exciting temptress who'd just kissed him, or this reticent young woman who looked as if she'd scared herself with her bold moves.

"You can change your mind," he said. "I should back out. This isn't the smartest thing I've ever done—"

"Shh," she interrupted, "stay in character, don't ruin the spell." Then she captured his mouth with hers again.

That was all it took. Testosterone surged through his body. His muscles tightened. His hands roved over the lush curve of her body, and he dipped his head to kiss her again. If she was in the mood for acting, then he was eager to comply. Whatever turned her on.

Wait, stop, you can't do this. Remember the morality clause you signed.

The words battered at the back of his hormone-laced brain, but they sounded very far away, like a cell phone call from a tunnel—his sensible side snuffed out by instinct and molten desire.

This was so unlike him, losing control, losing his head. And yet he couldn't deny the power of this attraction. It was nonsensical and scary as hell, but it was too real to deny. His muscles ached. His skin burned. His cock throbbed.

If he didn't get her into bed, he felt as if he just might die from the wanting, the craving, the hunger.

She gently bit his bottom lip and he almost groaned. Not because she'd hurt him, but because her boldness and his stark need blindsided him. Had he ever in his life been this turned on?

Beyond all reason, he had to have her.

WALKING INTO THE COTTAGE was like stepping back in time over four hundred years into a medieval love nest designed to stoke the senses.

Gorgeous velvet and damask tapestries, replicas of the Renaissance era, adorned the walls. The heavy mahogany sofa and chairs were padded and upholstered in rich, dark leather. The colors were equally strong and luxurious—crimson, gold, indigo, salmon. The gas-powered fireplace, complete with a sixteenth-century-style inglenook, had been lit. Apparently it was part of the turning-down service because a basket of goodies wrapped in red cellophane lay on the trestle table in the kitchenette.

Not that Roxie really noticed. She was too hung up on the raw sexual energy rolling off Shakespeare and zapping into her.

She wasn't sure why she was doing what she was doing. She'd never had a one-night stand or even a weekend fling, but this felt too right to be wrong. She only knew she had to have him. For once in her life, she was going with the flow and would float wherever the current carried her.

Of course, the current rolling off Dougal was more like a tidal wave, but instead of feeling scared as she normally would have, she felt wildly intrigued and uncharacteristically daring.

His hands were all over her body, but more than that, she was all over him. Kisses landed in various places, lips, noses, foreheads, chins. They pulled at each other's clothing, eager to get naked. She plucked at the buttons of his shirt; his fingers searched for the zipper of her frock. In a clumsy tango of entangled limbs, they stumbled from the sitting room into the bedroom.

They tumbled onto the solid oak, ornately carved four-poster bed sporting an elaborate canopy draped with more opulent fabrics. The linens had been turned down, and foil-wrapped chocolates rested on the pillows along with packets of condoms. Clearly they didn't call the resort Eros for nothing.

She was on her back, her skirt hiked up to her waist. Her sex was already slick for him.

The subtle sconce lighting cast his face in shadows. He looked savage, primitive. His cheekbones appeared razor sharp, his lips full and foreboding and his chin firm beneath the perfectly trimmed beard. This man was a stranger, but instead of being frightened, she was highly aroused. Her nipples pebbled, womb contracted, every nerve ending taking note of this very masculine male.

He didn't move, just stood there looking down at her until she suddenly felt self-conscious. She reached up to pull her skirt down over her thighs, but he restrained her.

"No, do not hide, milady." Dougal shook his head. "Your beauty outshines the sun. My eyes long to feast upon you."

Roxie's cheeks heated. She'd never felt particularly attractive. She had a crooked front tooth and her forehead was too short and her skin was too pale, and those extra five pounds she lugged around and couldn't seem to lose converged into a round little pooch at her belly.

But the look in his eyes made her feel beautiful, and the way he was speaking—as if he actually were Shakespeare—shoved her libido into overdrive.

"There is none so lovely as you," he murmured, and ran his palm up her calf to her knee.

She pressed her knees together, wanting him desperately, but suddenly afraid she was going to disappoint him.

He paused, held her gaze. "Your hair is the color of ink, so dark and mysterious against your creamy skin. And the way you move—soft as a sigh." His hand slipped higher, a coaxing finger circling her kneecap.

Every muscle in her body tensed, and she had to bite the inside of her cheek to keep from moaning.

His fingers kept tickling, exploring, teasing. She let her

knees drop outward, giving him easier access. He made a noise of satisfaction and massaged the back of her knee.

He must have hit some kind of trigger point because a sizzling red-hot wire of glorious sensation shot from her knee straight up into her clenched womb. Reflexively her hips arched up off the mattress.

What a feeling!

A desperate, keening cry slipped past her lips. Tossed like an airplane on a sudden updraft, she fisted her hands, gathering up handfuls of the brocade bedspread. His hand trailed farther up her right leg, his fingers gliding over her left.

He took her by the waist and moved her into the middle of the bed and then he was there beside her, spreading her legs apart, dipping his head, touching her with his lips, his tongue a torturous taskmaster. He inched his mouth from her ankles to her calf to her kneecap, commanding her to moan and squirm and beg.

This was the sexiest thing that had ever happened to her. She had no idea her toes and feet and legs were so sensitive, so desperate for attention. She was electrified.

He finished slipping off her costume, leaving her wearing only her panties and camisole and slowly stroked her bare midriff. His fingers brushed against her navel, enlivening things even more. He went back to kiss her leg, moving up her thigh. One hand was teasing her navel, the other hand rubbing the back of her kneecap.

Roxie was in turmoil. Helplessly she quivered in his arms. "My lord, this is not fair to thee."

"To what does my lady refer?"

"You are still cloaked while I am laid bare." She surprised herself by saying, "'Tis time for me to see your naked skin."

"These damnable boots," he muttered, and went to work on getting them unlaced. He stood up, kicked them off, and the boots were quickly followed by his pants.

They were left in their underwear, aware of nothing but each other, the sounds of their hungry gasps raspy in the darkened room.

Roxie hadn't seen very many naked men in real life. Her two boyfriends and that was it. And neither John nor Marcus could compare with the man in front of her. In a word, Dougal Lockhart was beefcake. Big and thick and well, just...*amazing*.

Looking at him made her want to do things she'd never done before. Bold things. Exciting things. Wild and adventuresome things. A dozen different emotions pelted her at once—titillation, eagerness, curiosity, giddiness, hope. Sensory input overwhelmed her—the sound of Dougal's ragged breathing, the heat of his flesh against hers, the scrape of his beard as he claimed her mouth in another kiss.

A maelstrom of wicked delight swept her away; a rushing river of passion surging high, increasing the sexual drive that had been building since their encounter on the plane. He tasted rich and tangy like some spicy, exotic dish. She hungered for more. The tender slide of his palms underneath her breasts as he made her camisole disappear became an urgent quest to increase her pleasure.

Roxie's nipples were rock hard, her breasts swollen and achy. She was dripping for him, juicy and ready.

Compelled by the burning urge to stroke him, to travel the tempting terrain of his body, she ran her fingertips over his belly. She exalted in the way his taut stomach muscles quivered at her touch.

His low groan of pleasure lit her up inside. She tracked her hand lower, finding her way through the coarse curls to glide her palm up the long, hard length of him.

Dougal's fiery gaze roved over her; his hands sent ribbons of pleasure unfurling throughout her body. "Woman, do you have any idea just how damned sexy you are?"

"Shakespeare." She breathed, tossed by her tumultuous thoughts. Longing overwhelmed her. She couldn't resist. He was so damned handsome with that shock of dark brown hair and his tanned skin.

When she reached up, threaded her arms around his neck and went in for another kiss, he smiled and languidly dipped his tongue into her mouth.

She strummed her tongue against his, making herself an active participant. If she was going to go through with this, then she was going to take full responsibility for what happened. Afterward she could tell herself she'd known exactly what she was doing. This time there would be no regrets. Roxie didn't stop him when his hand drifted to her panties.

"Lift up your hips, Muse," he commanded.

She obeyed, levering her lower back off the bed as his big hand made short work of the slight material.

He made a guttural sound low in his throat. This was it. No begging off now. He rolled to one side and stripped off his boxer briefs in a motion so practiced she had to wonder how many bedrooms he'd performed it in, how many other women he'd slept with. His erection burgeoned, thick and heavily veined, the velvety head purpled and pulsating.

"Oh, my." She inhaled audibly.

It was his turn to blush, which did a strange thing to her heart. He was shy with her, this big, commanding man.

She sat up and reached for him, but he grabbed her wrist to stop her. "No," he rasped. "If you touch me now I shall be ruined."

Lowering his head, he pressed his lips to her bare belly and kissed his way to her breasts, heavy and aching. She shivered.

"Pray tell me thy pleasure. It is my honor to do your bidding."

"Yes," was all she could manage to say.

He flicked his tongue over one nipple and lightly bit down.

Razor-thin shards of pleasure spread throughout her breast. She moaned.

"Does this please thee?" he asked.

"No."

"No?" He pulled back, looked confused.

"It exalts me."

He grinned and kept going, his mouth sucking, his tongue teasing, fingers tickling. Brilliant. Absolutely brilliant. He left her nipples and traveled downward, moving his tongue in a counterclockwise motion. The maneuver produced crazy, erotic ripples in her belly that undulated all the way down into her heated sex.

When his lips reached her throbbing clit, he stopped just short of touching her with his tongue. His breath was hot against her tender flesh, igniting her beyond reason. She arched her hips again, trying to bring his mouth and her clit into contact, but he moved with her, keeping his mouth just out of her reach.

"My lord does see fit to torture me," she said through gritted teeth.

He chuckled.

"You are unkind."

"Patience, Muse, patience."

She didn't want to hang on. She wanted him to love her with his mouth right this second. Her brain was glazed with lust, her body worked up to a fevered pitch.

Gently he spread her thighs wider and moved his body around so that he knelt between her legs. "Beautiful," he crooned.

The head of his penis pulsed against her knee as he leaned forward. Roxie's excitement escalated. She couldn't stand it. She'd never felt such desperate pressure.

His big fingers gently caressed her clit as his tongue probed her inner folds. Her eyes slid closed as she savored what he was doing to her.

"Please," she whimpered. "Please don't stop."

He captured her clit with his mouth. Never in all her life had she been pleasured this way. It was ecstasy. He seemed to know exactly what she wanted and needed, even before she did.

While he suckled her clit, he slipped a finger into her slick wetness. The walls of her sex sucked at his finger, gripping and kneading him in rhythmic waves, pulling him deeper and deeper into her.

Sound was altered and she existed in a delicious void, simply floating, aware of every physical sensation. "Mmm," he intoned. "You taste of nectar, hot and sweet."

She rode his tongue, got lost in it. She hovered on the brink of orgasm, but he would not let her fall over. A steady strumming vibration began deep in her throat and emerged as a wild moan.

"Please," she begged. "Please."

"Please what, Muse? You must request what you need."

"Please, please make me come."

He let loose then, gave her his all. His tongue danced, his fingers manipulated. She let go of all control and just allowed him to take over. It seemed he was everywhere—over her, around her, in her, outside of her. He was magic. He was amazing. And she was his instrument, tuned and ready to be played.

"More." She thrashed her head. "Harder."

He gave it to her just the way she asked for it, pumping his thick finger into her, while his tongue pressed the button of her release. "Come, Muse, come," he cajoled.

She came. Exploding in great, writhing pleasure. She gave a long, low cry. It flowed from her, the release she'd needed for years.

Shakespeare pulled her to him, cradling her to his chest as her ragged breathing returned to normal. Roxie couldn't stop a spontaneous grin from spreading across her face.

"Why are you smiling, Muse?" he asked, leaning over to

brush her lips with his. Lying here with her calmed him in a way he'd never quite felt before. Roxie was as soothing as a soak in a hot tub, and playing this little Shakespeare game with her had been incredibly erotic.

"Oh, now you're angling for compliments," she teased.

"I just wanted to share in the joke."

"Believe me, big man, that was no joke."

He reached up to push aside a strand of hair that had fallen over her forehead. "You enjoyed it?" he felt compelled to ask, and then immediately regretted it. He didn't want her to think she needed to bolster his self-esteem on that score, but the truth was, it had been a very long time since he'd been with a woman and he was a little unsure of himself.

She looked up at him with those wide, vulnerable blue eyes that yanked on his heartstrings. What was it about her that got to him on such a primal level? "That's the first time…um… er…no one's ever…"

"Made love to you with their mouth?" he finished for her.

Even in the dimmed lighting, he could see her blush. "Yeah, that."

A thrill shot through him. Okay, maybe it was a bit chauvinistic, but he liked that he was the first to give her oral sex. "So what do you think? How was it?"

"If it wasn't for the fact that *you* got nothing out of the deal, I'd say chuck the whole intercourse thing and stick with oral sex."

"There are two things about that statement that bother me," he said. "One, nothing is better than good, old-fashioned sex, that is if you're doing it right, and two, I got plenty out of it. Knowing that I'm making you feel good charges me up."

"The male pride thing, huh?"

"Exactly, and besides, we're just getting started." He kissed her softly. "By the time this evening is over—"

The sound of his cell phone trilling the specialized ring tone he'd programmed to play when the resort's security staff called interrupted him. Much as he wanted to ignore it, he couldn't.

"Excuse me a minute," he said, slipping out from under her.

Roxie gave a soft noise of disappointment.

"I'll be right back." Dougal leaned over to kiss the tip of her nose. "Don't go anywhere."

He found his pants on the floor and fished his cell phone from the back pocket. "Hello?"

"Mr. Lockhart, this is Gerry McCracken."

Dougal had met Gerry and the other members of resort security after he'd arrived, and he'd held a small conference meeting, telling them to be hypervigilant concerning anything suspicious, but he'd stopped short of relating the details about a possible saboteur. Even though Taylor put her employees through a rigorous background check, Dougal was by nature a suspicious man. It took a lot for him to trust people, even those he'd known a long time.

And yet, within hours after meeting her, you've bedded Roxanne Stanley.

"What's up?" he asked Gerry, waving to Roxie as he padded out of the bedroom, cell phone pressed to his ear.

She waved back.

"I smell rotten fish in Denmark," Gerry said.

Dougal stepped into the sitting area, shutting the bedroom door behind him. His gut clenched, knowing from the sound of Gerry's voice that he was going to confirm what Dougal suspected. "What did you find out?"

"I was investigatin' why the spotlight fell, and I noticed all the nuts were missin' from the mountin' bolts. I thought you might wanna come see for yourself."

Alarm raced up Dougal's spine. "I'll be right there."

"I'M SORRY," DOUGAL SAID as he wrestled into his clothes. "I have to go."

"What's wrong?" Roxie sat up in bed, her legs curled underneath her, the sheet drawn up to cover her nakedness. She felt suddenly shy in spite of what he'd just done to her with his wicked mouth and tongue.

"Um…tour-guide emergency." An odd look passed over his face and as soon as he said it, she knew he was lying.

"What kind of emergency does a tour guide have in the middle of the night?" she asked, insecurity grabbing hold of her.

"You know…disgruntled guests." He sat on the edge of the bed, jammed his feet into his boots and began lacing them up.

"Can't the concierge handle it?" Why was she pushing this? If the man wanted to leave, she should let him leave. That was the logical conclusion to a one night stand. If she was going to play the game, she had to accept the rules. Except she'd gotten off and he hadn't. What guy left before he'd claimed his orgasm?

"I'm afraid not." He got up. "I don't want you to think I'm running out on you."

"But you are."

"Yeah, but it's got nothing to do with you. Duty calls."

Right. She ducked her head. She shouldn't have any expectations from this man. Easy come, easy go. Pun intended.

He leaned over the bed, cupped his palm under her chin, and tilted her face up to meet his gaze. "Hey."

"Yes?"

"You and I need to talk."

"There's nothing to talk about. I'm fine." She waved, tried to ignore the gentle pressure on her chin and how good it felt to be touched by him. "Go, do your thing."

"I wouldn't be leaving if this wasn't important."

"It's okay."

"It's not okay. Listen…" He inhaled, met her gaze. "I don't

want you to think I go around doing this sort of thing. I don't. I'm not a casual guy. Not about my work, not about my relationships, certainly not about sex."

"You don't have to explain yourself to me."

"I want to explain myself to you, dammit," he snapped.

"Sorry, I didn't mean to irritate."

"You didn't irritate me. I just wanted you to understand." His voice and expression softened. "I'm not a casual guy. I don't get swept away by my passion."

"And yet you did."

"And yet I did," he echoed.

Roxie raised her palms as a strange emotion she couldn't identify slithered through her. "Whoa."

"Yeah," he whispered. "Whoa."

"Listen," they said in unison and then laughed.

"You first." He nodded.

"I came on this trip to let loose, let go, explore my…um…" Roxie hesitated. She wasn't completely lying. Sure her boss had sent her to spy on Eros, but she had her own agenda, as well. She wanted to make up for lost time, let her hair down, have some fun, find out what she'd been missing.

"Sexuality."

"Yeah, that. I've been sheltered and I figured it was time I saw what the world has to offer."

He nodded. "That's the reason everyone comes to an Eros resort."

They stared in each other's eyes.

"What we just did," he went on, "well, I violated all the rules. There's no excuse for it. I crossed the line. But here's the funny thing—I'm a big stickler for the rules. I don't break them and yet one kiss from you and my brain short-circuited."

"What rules?" she whispered, thrilling to his words. She'd

never driven a man to break the rules before and it was a heady rush.

"It's in my contract. A morality clause. No fraternizing with the guests."

"We just fraternized," she pointed out.

"Big-time."

"So what does this mean?"

"I can't, I shouldn't…this needs to…"

"Stop?" She arched an eyebrow.

"Yeah."

Disappointment arrowed through her. She'd known being with Dougal was too good to be true. So much for her wild vacation fling.

"But I don't want it to stop," he murmured.

"What are you saying?" She lowered her voice, both intrigued and titillated.

"We shouldn't take this any further."

"No." She nodded as if she meant yes.

Dougal's hand was still on her chin, his eyes locked on hers. "But this chemistry between us…" He shook his head. "Wow."

"Wow," she echoed.

"If it was another time, another place, we'd owe it to ourselves to fully explore it."

"We would."

"It might even have been the best sex of our lives."

"I have no doubt." The way he looked at her sent blood pumping hot and thick straight to her groin.

"I really do have to go now," he said. "Tomorrow on the tour—"

"Got it. Act like nothing happened."

7

DOUGAL COULDN'T BELIEVE what he'd just done. This was so unlike him. He wasn't a rebel, no rule breaker, and yet the thought of an illicit affair with Roxie excited him as nothing ever had.

What was it about her that turned him inside out? It was more than just that rich ebony hair and those impossibly blue eyes. More than just her porcelain skin and lush, curvy body. It was in the way she looked at him, full of trust and admiration. She made him feel strong and honorable and heroic, and he had an overwhelming urge to live up to all of her expectations.

How had this happened? What did it mean? Startled, he stepped back from the bed. "Sleep well," he mumbled.

"Until tomorrow," she whispered.

Dougal left the cottage, rushed up the cobblestone walkway and into the castle, his heart thumping fast and hard.

Gerry McCracken was in the dining room with a few members of the cleaning staff when Dougal arrived, mentally muddled and emotionally sheepish. The minute Gerry spied him, he stalked over, hands on his hips, his shock of carrot-colored hair mussed as if he'd been repeatedly running his fingers through it. He sized up Dougal with a sidelong look. "Did I interrupt you in the middle of something?"

"Um...no," Dougal lied. "Why would you ask that?"

"Your shirt's buttoned up wrong." The Scotsman, who

was almost as tall as Dougal, smirked. "Sorry to be spoilin' your evenin'."

"Let's take a look at the stage lights." Dougal hastily unbuttoned his shirt and buttoned it up again and followed Gerry to the metal staircase leading to the overhead scaffolding.

They both had to lower their heads as they made their way up, and then crouch and duckwalk as the space grew narrower where the lights were mounted.

"See here," Gerry said, pointing out the studs in the bracket that had once held the spotlight that had crashed onto the stage. "Studs are intact."

"Meaning they didn't break off." Dougal stroked his beard with his thumb and index finger. He moved over to take a look at the remaining spotlights. They all had washers with self-locking nuts. No way could the nuts on the one that had fallen come off by themselves.

"I'm thinkin' someone loosened all the nuts until they were held on by just one thread, so it held for a while until the pressure from the weight of the spotlight popped them off."

"If that's the case, the nuts will be around here somewhere. Let's go back down and check the stage."

Ten minutes later, they'd found all eight nuts, and Dougal wore gloves to collect them in a plastic bag to keep from obliterating any fingerprints that might be on them. This was clearly no accident.

Gerry looked at the wing nuts, shook his head. "There's no doubt about it, Dougal. This was sabotage."

Dougal had to agree and that meant calling Taylor. He excused himself and headed outside to make the call. He couldn't stop his gaze from straying to Roxie's cottage. The lights were out. Random thoughts roamed through his mind. Was she naked under the covers? Was she thinking of him?

Thinking of him and touching herself the way he wanted to think of her and touch himself?

Stop it! Don't get sidetracked.

Purposely he shook off his unprofessional fantasies and punched in Taylor's number. When she answered, he told her what had happened with the spotlight. "This definitely looks deliberate."

Taylor made a noise of concern. "I heard back from the mechanics about the autopilot on the plane."

"And?"

"The results were inconclusive."

"Meaning it may or may not have been an accident."

"Yes."

Dougal cleared his throat. "Taylor," he said, "I've been thinking and I'm not sure I'm the right person for this job."

"What do you mean? You're the perfect person for the job."

"There's someone on the tour…." What was he going to say? That something about Roxie raised his suspicions at the very same time his gut was telling him she couldn't possibly be a saboteur? He had no proof to go on, and honestly, if she was the culprit, why would she risk standing under the spotlight she'd loosened?

"That's got all your senses on alert?" Taylor supplied.

That was certainly true. "Yes."

"You suspect this person?"

Dougal drew in a deep breath. How did you tell your boss that you'd already broken the morality clause you'd signed and you'd broken it with your prime suspect. "I don't know."

"Is it a woman?"

"Yes," he said.

"And you're attracted to her?"

"I am," he said.

"You don't seem like the kind of guy who would renege on an agreement," Taylor said.

"I'm not reneging. I just don't think I can be objective about this person."

"What makes you say that?"

"She was a volunteer in the Shakespeare skit and she, um…kissed me."

"And you felt things."

He didn't deny it. "So you see why I need to excuse myself from the case."

"Don't be ridiculous," Taylor said.

"What do you mean?" Dougal frowned and paced the cobblestone walkway.

"If she is the saboteur and she's attracted to you, this gives you the perfect opportunity to get close to her, get her to let down her guard and confess her sins to you."

You have no idea how close I've already gotten to her.

"Just don't act on the attraction. If word got out that members of my staff were sleeping with the guests…well, let's just say it would be a PR nightmare. But I do encourage you to string her along, keep her wanting more."

This is the time. Tell her you've already acted on it.

But for some reason, Dougal simply couldn't force himself to say the words. Part of his silence was a misguided attempt at chivalry. Part of it was because he felt ashamed for losing control so easily. He also didn't want to disappoint Taylor.

"Don't let this attraction throw you. You're a strong man both physically and mentally," Taylor said. "You can get close to her and determine if she could be our suspect without letting your feelings take over. You learned your lesson in Germany, did you not?"

"I did."

That, Dougal realized, was the real reason he didn't tell

Taylor the whole truth about what he'd just done to Roxie in her bedroom. When it came down to it, this assignment was all about proving that he had learned from his mistakes.

"Dougal," Taylor said, "just find who is undermining my resorts by any means possible."

ROXIE COULDN'T SLEEP. If it wasn't so late, she'd go knock on Sam and Jess's door and ask for advice on how to keep casual sex casual.

But it was almost three o'clock in the morning, and Dougal had been gone for hours. Already she missed him.

This wasn't good. Not good at all.

And she was wallowing in a hole in the bed from all her tossing and turning. She might as well get up and take a moonlit walk in the gardens. Maybe the fresh air would clear her feverish head.

She got dressed, slipped on a light sweater and stepped out to stroll the cobblestones. She kept thinking about Dougal. Emotions overwhelmed her. She felt thunderstruck, inquisitive, voracious, jubilant, empowered and amorous all at once. Good feelings, euphoric feelings, but very scary. She wanted to hop up and down and clap her hands like a six-year-old at her birthday party.

At last.

The thought hung in her mind. She didn't know what it meant; she simply felt it in every part of her body.

At last.

At last what? That she was finally exploring the sexuality she'd hidden down deep inside her while she'd raised Stacy? At last she'd found a guy who didn't mind role-playing with her? At last…

She didn't really want to follow that thought to all the places it could lead because she knew she was vulnerable. Knew

Dougal was the kind of guy she could fall in love with. Especially since she had no experience with keeping things casual. She trailed through the garden, the air heavy with the scent of flowers and dew collecting on her slippers.

So what was she to do? Forget about all the delicious promise inherent in a fling, or take the plunge and risk getting her heart broken? She plunked down on a cement bench at the back of the garden and pondered the question under the glow of the moon.

Maybe you don't have to get your heart broken, whispered the quiet voice at the back of her mind. *If you just keep playacting, maybe you can have your sex and keep your heart intact.*

If she pretended to be someone else and donned a new persona every time she was with Dougal, she wouldn't be the one falling for him. It would be the muse falling for Shakespeare or Lady Chatterley falling for the stableman or Elizabeth Bennet falling for Mr. Darcy.

What an appealing idea.

Roxie made up her mind and arose from the park bench with fresh waves of excitement washing over her. That's exactly what she was going to do. Meanwhile, she had a job to do for Porter Langley and since she couldn't get to sleep, now was a perfect time to do a little snooping.

THE NEXT MORNING, Roxie climbed onboard the tour bus headed for an excursion throughout the English countryside. Today she was Lady Chatterley and Dougal was Oliver.

"Hello, good morning, welcome aboard." Dougal greeted her just as he'd greeted every other guest boarding the bus.

Roxie did not linger near him, although she longed to do so. She caught a whiff of his cologne and the spicy, masculine smell immediately filled her mind with images of the previous night. Ducking her head to hide the pink flush burning her cheeks, she headed for the long bench seat at back of the bus, figuring it was safest to put as much distance between Lady Chatterley and Oliver as possible.

She'd just sat down when Jess and Sam plunked into the seat beside her, chattering nonstop. "So what happened last night?" Jess asked.

"Happened?" Roxie fiddled with the strap of her purse.

"You know, with Mr. Handsome, after the spotlight fell," Sam added.

"Um...nothing happened."

"That wasn't what we were reading from his body language," Jess said. "That man is seriously into you."

Be cool. Don't give yourself away.

"Is he?" she said mildly. "I hadn't noticed."

"Woman, you need to make an appointment with an ophthalmologist because you're going blind. When you two are near each other, the rest of us can practically see the smoke rising off you," Sam said.

From his place at the front of the bus, Dougal was regaling the group with saucy tales of legendary lovers throughout British history. His eyes landed on her. Quickly Roxie jerked her gaze away.

"See," Jess crowed. "That right there." She made a hissing noise like the sound of bacon hitting a hot griddle. "Sizzle."

"I think we're making her uncomfortable," Sam said at Roxie's fidgeting.

"Oh, sorry," Jess apologized. "I was just teasing."

Roxie quickly changed the subject.

For their first stop of the day, the tour visited an estate in Derbyshire. Reportedly it was the site of D. H. Lawrence's fictional tale of *Lady Chatterley's Lover.* Dougal herded the group through the house, and then thirty minutes later, he led them to the stables.

"Anyone who's read the book knows this is the setting of some of the most erotic scenes in classic literature," he said.

Roxie lifted her head to find him staring straight at her. Feeling decidedly unsettled, she flicked out the tip of her tongue to whisk away a tiny pearl of perspiration that had suddenly beaded on her upper lip.

"I haven't read the book," Sam said. "Can you fill us in?"

"Let's just say there's a reason haylofts have come to signify passion in the countryside," Dougal explained.

This brought suggestive comments from the crowd.

The air inside the barn smelled earthy, musty, lusty. Dust motes danced on a shaft of sunlight. Saddles and horse blankets and leather riding crops hung on the walls. Cameras clicked as everyone vied for the best shot. Jess and Sam mugged it up in comically sexy poses with some guys they'd met on the tour.

Unbidden, Roxie imagined that it was she and Dougal making good use of the hayloft and its intriguing accoutrements. She gulped at the fantasy of his long, tanned fingers caressing her body.

"Ultimately," he said, his tone of voice stroking something deep inside Roxie, "Lawrence's book is about Connie's realization that she cannot live by her mind alone, that she must be sexually active to remain vital. As Oliver and Connie's relationship develops, she learns that sex is nothing to be ashamed of, while he learns about the spiritual challenges that come from sexual love."

Roxie knew it was a canned speech, but Dougal's eyes smoldered. All she could think about was getting him into bed again. The events from last night kept circling her brain, tossing her thoughts around like a tumultuous tornado.

For the remainder of the tour, she avoided meeting his eyes, but she couldn't shake the scent of him from her nostrils. By the time the tour was over, Roxie's skin ached hot and raw; her imagination was a fertile and dangerous erotic playground. In the ladies' room, she dampened a paper towel and pressed it against the nape of her neck.

"Are you okay?" Sam asked.

Roxie forced a smile. "I'm fine."

"Are you sure?" Jess piped up. "Your cheeks are flushed."

"And your eyes are shiny," Sam added. "Do you have a fever?" She made a move as if she was going to put her hand to Roxie's forehead to check.

Roxie stepped back. "No, no, I just got a bit—" she paused, searching for the right word "—overheated in the hayloft."

"Didn't we all?" Jess fanned herself with a hand. "Dougal sure made *Lady Chatterley's Lover* come alive."

Jealousy bit into her. She knew most of the women on the tour were lusting after him, but she didn't want to hear about it.

"But Dougal only has eyes for Roxie," Sam said.

Roxie washed her hands. She dashed out into the hall and almost ran smack-dab into Dougal's hard, muscled chest.

"Whoa," he said, reaching out a hand to slow her forward momentum. "Where's the gold rush?"

Flustered, she sidled away from him. "Sorry."

"No need to apologize."

She didn't look at him, but she could feel his eyes on her.

Once everyone had rejoined the group, Dougal said, "Let's head back to the bus. Next stop is lunch at Tom Jones Tavern."

Forty minutes later they arrived at a quaint little pub on the outskirts of a picturesque village. Just before he signaled for the driver to let them off the bus, Dougal sauntered down the aisle passing out orange plastic tags with numbers printed on them. "We're mixing things up for this meal," he said. "The numbers on the tags correspond with a seating chart inside the restaurant. A stimulating vacation pushes you out of your comfort zone and that's what's happening today. So go find your seats and enjoy meeting new friends."

A murmur ran through the crowd at this turn of events.

The bus doors whispered open and by the time the front of the bus emptied, Dougal had made it to the back. He passed the last two tags out to Jess and Sam.

"We'll see you inside." Sam waved to Roxie and then turned to follow her twin sister off the bus.

"Will you look at that," Dougal said, holding out his open palms. "I've run out of tags. Looks like you'll just have to sit with me."

"You did that on purpose," she said.

"It's the only way to have lunch with you without calling attention to our having lunch together." He leveled a seductive smile at her. She thought about last night and a shiver raced down her spine.

"Are you sure it's wise to risk it?"

"Wise?" He arched an eyebrow. "Probably not."

"But you're going to do it anyway?"

"I can't seem to stay away from you."

Roxie was flattered. She'd never had a guy flirt with her like this. Then again, she usually did her best to avoid male attention. Normally it made her uncomfortable. The fact that she was enjoying this banter with Dougal was quite telling indeed. The Gordian knot in her stomach tightened.

Once inside the pub, they took the last remaining booth tucked into a darkened corner away from the majority of the diners. On the flat-screen television above the bar, the eating scene from the movie *Tom Jones* played out its lusty message of culinary excess. Menus lay on the table. She picked one up and studied it.

Dougal folded his hands and sat watching her. After a moment, she glanced up from the menu and forced herself to meet his gaze. "I have a yearning for a nice, juicy turkey leg. What are you getting?"

"I'm tempted to say oysters." His gaze flicked to the on-screen movie snippet where the actors were in the midst of seducing each other with raw oysters. "But that would be too obvious." His own lusty smile heated her from the inside out. "I think I'll join you and have the turkey leg, as well."

His eyes snagged her gaze and held it over the flicking candles secured with wax into the necks of empty ale bottles. The walls were constructed of knotty pine, the floors of centuries-old planks. Food was served in trenchers instead of on plates, the drinks in pewter mugs. The rustic decor, along with the scent of roasting meat, had the intended effect—basic, raw, sexy.

The waitress, decked out in a serving wench costume, appeared at their table. "What'll you two be 'avin'?" she asked, hamming up the Cockney accent.

"Two turkey-leg lunches." Dougal ordered for them both. "With all the trimmings. I'll have a lager and she'll have…" He paused, raised his eyebrow at her.

"I'll have a lager, too," she said. Why not? She was on vacation.

After the waitress left, Roxie leaned forward to whisper, "Are you sure we should be doing this so out in the open?"

"Is there a better way to conduct a secret affair? No one suspects if you're open about it."

"Are we having a secret affair?"

"You tell me."

"Aren't you afraid of losing your job?"

"I'm more afraid of losing the chance to get to know you better."

That surprised and embarrassed her a bit. She'd never had a man come on so strong. And she liked it. Was that bad? "Really?"

His eyes were warm. "Really."

"Still, I'd feel guilty." She glanced around the room, but no one seemed to be paying them any attention. That helped her to relax a little. She sank against the back of the booth. "If you got into trouble…"

"Let me worry about that."

Roxie didn't know what to say. Her body yearned for his touch and getting to know him was a smart thing in regard to her reason for being here. Surely he possessed insider information she could pass along to her boss, but the thought of using him left a bad taste in her mouth.

Dougal leaned back, mirroring her movements. "So," he said, "tell me more about Roxanne Stanley."

"I'm pretty boring, actually," she confessed. "You already know I love emocore, chicken Marsala and walnut brownies and that I'm an executive assistant. I'm originally from Albany, but I moved to Brooklyn when I got a job in the city. That pretty well covers me."

"What about your parents, your siblings?"

Roxie drew in a deep breath. Even though it had been ten years, she still hurt to think about her parents. "My folks were killed in a car crash when I was eighteen and my little sister, Stacy, was eight."

He looked genuinely sympathetic. "I'm sorry to hear that. I apologize for prying. I didn't mean to stir up bad memories. You don't have to tell me anything else."

"It's okay." She told him about Stacy, how she'd raised her alone. "I couldn't bear the thought of sending her to live with distant relatives or worse, having her end up in foster care. We're really close."

"That must have been really hard on you."

"You'd think so, but honestly we didn't notice. We had each other and we had a lot of fun together. Because I was so young myself, I let her do things like have ice cream for breakfast once a week and on Saturdays we'd spend the day in our pajamas."

"A girlie version of Neverland?"

"Something like that. Plus we had friends and neighbors that helped us. The experience taught me people are basically very good at heart. Of course, growing up with parents who ran a dinner theater had already given me a cheery, soft-focus view of the world. We were always playing or singing or watching upbeat movies together."

"So that's where you got your acting talent. It sounds like a nice way to grow up," he said.

"It was. The biggest adjustment for me was moving to the city and figuring out not everyone was as kind and welcoming as the people I'd grown up around. Even so, I've met more nice people than rude ones, but I've been accused of wearing rose-colored glasses. The criticism doesn't bother me. I believe people and places live up to your expectations. How about you?" she asked. "Where are you from?"

He made a face. "I don't like to talk about my childhood."

"Hey, that's not fair. You can't leave me hanging. I opened up to you. For this to be a real conversation you have to reciprocate."

"You're right." He shifted in his seat, then paused a moment before saying, "I was born in Detroit, on the wrong side of the tracks."

"I've heard Detroit is a tough town."

"It can be."

"Do your parents still live there?"

His eyes darkened. "My father took off when I was eight. I haven't seen him since."

She saw the long-ago pain of being abandoned by his father flicker in his eyes, but it quickly disappeared. "What about your mom?"

"After my dad left, she was a wreck. She took up with the

first guy who came along. He turned out to be a con man who took her life savings." Dougal clenched his teeth. The muscle at his jaw jumped.

Roxie reached out to touch his hand. "You felt responsible, like you should have protected her."

"Yeah," he admitted, then offered her a fleeting smile. "I blamed myself. I wondered what I'd done to chase my father off."

"You were just a kid. Kids blame themselves for things beyond their control."

"I know."

"But it still haunts you."

"You're too perceptive for my own good, Roxanne Stanley."

"So how's your mom now?"

"Good. She moved to Florida to take care of my grandmother when I joined the Air Force and signed up for officer's training. After my grandmother died, she started her own business, a transportation company that chauffeurs the elderly and disabled to where they need to go."

"You must be proud of her."

"I am. She's a strong woman."

"Through the Air Force you got to see the world."

"I did."

"I'm jealous. Until I moved to Brooklyn, I'd never been out of Albany."

"Have you traveled much since then?"

"I went to Atlantic City once and the Catskills."

"That's it?"

"I'm here now."

"So this is Roxie's big adventure." His gaze was heated.

The waitress returned with their food and drink order. Roxie took a big swallow of lager and cast about for something to say to get her mind off the hot, tingling firing along her nerve endings.

Dougal picked up a piece of thick black bread and began buttering it. "Although I'm not sure how smart it is to take off across the Atlantic on your own."

"I'm not on my own. I'm with a tour group."

"But we're all strangers to you."

"Anyone can betray you—strangers, acquaintances, friends. You can't live your life being afraid of getting deceived. I know we've just met, but I get the feeling you're a pretty suspicious guy," she said, but then she reminded herself he had every right to be suspicious, especially where she was concerned. Like it or not, she was a spy. She kept forgetting that. While she wasn't doing anything illegal, she was certain that Taylor Corben would consider her conduct unethical. Plus, spying went against Roxie's own moral code and she wished she wasn't in a position to have to do it. She bit down on her bottom lip thinking of the photos she'd snapped of the resort during the middle of the night and had e-mailed to her boss. She hadn't exposed anything yet, but she knew he'd pressure her for more.

"You're right."

"You've been betrayed?"

"Haven't we all?"

"If you ever want to talk about it…" She shrugged. Why was she trying to get close to him? She should take Jess's advice and keep the personal information to a minimum. With his eagle-eyed gaze and leery nature, he stood a good chance of figuring out what she was really doing here. "I've been told I'm a good listener."

"Thanks for the offer," he murmured, but his eyes said, *There's no way in hell I'm taking you up on it.*

And Roxie couldn't help wondering why she suddenly felt so sad for him.

8

_____

AFTER LUNCH, THE TOUR headed to some ancient Roman ruins. The sky had grown overcast and the air hung damp and gloomy. They drove for over an hour and then passed a small village. The bus took a corner near a pub and souvenir shop, then ambled along the road curving up a rolling hillside. From out of nowhere, imposing rock ruins rose out of the bucolic English countryside.

Tiny blue butterflies basked on colorful flowers sprouting amidst the stone walls. Yellowhammers and greenfinches darted among the hedgerows. A magical place straight out of the storybooks layered with detailed history.

Dougal regaled them with stories about the Roman invasion of Britain in 43 AD, and Roxie's imagination stirred. He led them through the ruins to find a small stone church on the other side. "The church is believed to have been built in the twelfth century, over six hundred years after the Romans abandoned this location for reasons unknown. It was erected over a Roman temple using the original stones."

They moved away from the church, down a grassy green slope toward a small stream babbling over rocks. There lay an ancient cemetery, dark tombstones sticking up in the gathering fog.

"There's also a romantic legend attached to this cemetery." Dougal pointed out a gravestone. "It centers on a brave knight, Sir Gareth, who fell in love at first sight with lovely Sarah Mead, the daughter of the local lord. But alas, she was betrothed to another. To be together, they were forced to meet in secret in the bell tower of the church. There on the eve of Sarah's wedding to another man, they consummated their love."

It was fascinating stuff, but not as fascinating as the man doing the talking. His incredible body was too distracting for words. Roxie kept imagining she and Dougal were those star-crossed lovers. He was a stalwart knight and she was a maiden in a fix, doing the forbidden by following her heart. Desire held her tightly in its grip, and she couldn't shake the thought of making love to Dougal in that bell tower just as the young lovers had done centuries before.

"The lord's men caught them in the act, and he had the knight beheaded and his daughter banished to a nunnery. Distraught over losing her one true love, the grief-stricken Sarah took her own life," he continued.

Emotion hit low in Roxie's stomach. History was filled with such cruel stories about couples who'd gambled it all on love and lost not only each other, but their lives.

Romantic sentiment overwhelmed her as she thought of the past. She wanted to feel passion like that. Her gaze strayed to Dougal.

His eyes were on her.

Her pulse raced and in that moment she *was* Lady Sarah and he was Sir Gareth.

Dougal moistened his lips with the tip of his tongue.

Excitement she'd never felt before blazed through her. She had to do something about this neediness inside her or go mad. *The bell-tower church*, she thought. It was the perfect place to be alone and fantasize that she and Dougal were those doomed lovers.

Or better yet, entice him into making love to her right here.

DOUGAL WAS DOING HIS BEST to keep his mind on the task at hand and off Roxie, but he wasn't having much luck. As he talked, his gaze traveled over the bodice of Roxie's dress. She leaned over to study a headstone, enhancing his view of her cleavage. He took in the rounded swell of her breasts, her luminous skin.

She cast him a sideways glance and that's when he realized she was purposely letting him see straight down the opening of her top. She was teasing him, the little minx. The realization shot hot lust clean though his bones.

He couldn't make himself look away. Not even when he fumbled over the story. He'd been wound up tight as a coil ever since last night when he'd tasted her womanly sweetness. It was a flavor he craved again and again.

She lowered her lashes and stepped away from the group. He tracked her steps, struggling not to be obvious about watching her. Where was she going?

For a whisper of a second, she stopped, cast a look at him over her shoulder, then she moved toward the church. Almost instantly the fog swallowed her up.

He had to know where she was headed, what she was up to. Quickly he finished the tale of the mournful lovers. "Feel free to explore on your own," he said. "There are supplies for gravestone rubbings inside the bus if anyone is interested, or if you feel like walking, you can take tea at the pub we passed on the way in and browse the souvenir shop. It's a quarter of a mile to the end of the road and you have an hour before the bus leaves."

Without another word, he left the group standing where they were and went off after Roxie. It was stupid and he knew it, but he was compelled by a force he could neither control nor explain. He caught a glimpse of her dress as she disappeared behind a large headstone and the very air seemed to quiver with her spirited sexuality, beckoning him to follow.

He wove through the graveyard in hot pursuit. He was breathless but not from exertion—he was an athlete after all.

Rather it was excitement that stole the oxygen from his lungs. Stark physical need was a solid hand, reaching out to grab him.

Where was she? Which way had she gone?

There. Around the back of the old church. He spied a flash of her blue dress. She'd gone inside.

The fist of excitement tightened.

He continued to trace her steps and inhaled the now-familiar scent of her honeysuckle perfume. Stepping over the threshold into the crumbling shelter, he was just in time to see her disappear through the archway leading to the main part of the church. Did she know he was following her?

The thought that she was luring him inside for a delicious and unexpected seduction sent a shock of lust to his groin. With a grin of anticipation spreading across his face, he rushed after her.

ROXIE HEARD DOUGAL'S footsteps behind her. Her heart jackhammered at the hollow of her throat. She pressed her body flat against the stone wall of the chapel, just inside the archway. The pews stretched out ahead of her, leading to the altar. A hot, heavy feeling pushed through her lower abdomen, suffusing her sex with a persistent throb.

Hiding from him turned her on in a way she had not expected.

Dougal came barreling through the door so fast he didn't see her standing just to the side of the entrance. He took several long-legged strides away from her, heading for the exit behind the altar.

Pulse pounding, Roxie spun away from the wall and headed back out the archway he'd just come through, her shoes echoing loudly against the stone. She had no doubt that he'd heard her. Thrilled yet oddly terrified, she ran for the spiral staircase leading to an upper level. She had no plans, no idea what she was intending. Primal instinct drove her, the feminine urge to tease and seduce.

Immediately his footsteps changed directions; he was in pursuit of her again. Her mouth went dry as adrenaline surged, sending a metallic taste spilling into her mouth.

The game was on.

Feeling wild and free and crazy, she took the steps two at a time. She had never done anything like this and she gloried in the feelings vibrating through her. She had the distinct impression that Dougal, too, was enjoying the chase.

Exhilaration burned her cheeks. A tangle of images filled her mind, all of them erotic and involving unorthodox uses of a church. She reached the top of the stairs and entered the bell tower, blood whooshing loudly in her ears.

The tower was a big open room, the bell long gone. There was nowhere to hide. That's when she realized that the footsteps behind her had stopped.

Had Dougal given up, or had some members of the tour appeared in the church and halted the game?

She turned, walked back to the head of the stairs and cautiously peered down.

Dougal lounged on the staircase with his shoulder propped against the wall, arms folded over his chest, his eyes half-closed, an insouciant grin on his face.

She sprang back from the opening. The scrape of his shoes on the staircase sent gooseflesh up her arm. He was coming after her again and there was nowhere to run.

You started it.

Yeah, but she hadn't given much thought to finishing it.

She stood motionless, her skin smoldering, her body a five-alarm blaze. What was he going to do to her when he got up here?

Was he as excited as she? Did he have an erection? Was chasing her driving him as crazy as hiding from him was driving her? Her breasts grew heavy with longing.

His dark head crested the top of the stairs, followed by the rest of him. The sleeves of his shirt were rolled up to reveal his tanned arms roped with muscles. The foggy mist had curled his hair into ringlets at the back of his neck. He looked provocative in his costume of white shirt and black leather pants—basic, masculine, romantic. A whiff of his scent wafted over to her.

They did not speak. Roxie stood in the middle of the room, trembling with anticipation, her mind racing to guess what was going to happen next.

Then, with a noise of intense masculine desire, he crossed the room in a few strides. Roxie turned to flee, but found herself backed into a corner. She spun around to face him.

She was watching him and he was watching her. They sucked in rough, tandem gulps of oxygen.

The wrenching tug of jitters pulled her toward him at the same time it scared her deeply. She'd never felt this level of sexual arousal, this variety of achy sensitivity. Her body demanded release and he held the key.

Dougal gathered her into his arms and kissed her as if it was the last kiss he would ever receive.

The idea that they could be caught at any minute, that one of the other Eros guests could wander into the church and up the bell tower, escalated their cravings.

"We have to be quick about it," he rasped.

"Yes, yes, quick and hard," she agreed, barely recognizing herself but loving this new, brazen Roxie.

Dougal grasped her by the waist, turned her around. "Hands on the wall," he commanded.

Heart thudding, she obeyed, splaying her palms against the cool stone wall, her muscles tensing in shivery expectation. Reverentially, Dougal's hands skimmed over her body as if he loved the feel of her beneath him, as if she was a special gift he couldn't wait to unwrap.

He squashed his chest against her back, pressed his mouth to her ears and murmured sweet nothings as his hand dipped down to the hem of her skirt and his fingers slid up her quivering thigh.

Arching her back into him, she moaned softly against his tender stroking. He kissed the nape of her neck and breathed her name on a sigh.

"Doth my stalwart knight wear protection?" she whispered.

He groaned. "No."

Disappointment arrowed through her.

"Worry not, Lady Sarah," he said, role-playing with her as he'd done the evening before. "Your pleasure is my command."

Huh?

He tightened his grip around her waist and ground her bottom against his crotch. "My lady," he whispered, "there is none as captivating as you."

Roxie whimpered.

Dougal used his knee to spread her legs wider. He flipped the hem of her skirt up over her ass and with one swift move, pulled down her panties. He held her steady with one hand, while his other hand rubbed her cheeks, then he inched his hand lower and slipped inquisitive fingers between her legs. Playfully he swatted her fanny.

She hissed in air.

"Does that please my lady?"

She nodded, unable to speak.

Lightly he swatted her once more, the smack of his palm against her butt creating a very sexy sound in the cavernous room. The torturous pressure inside her womb twisted. How she wanted him inside her!

"Beautiful." His fingers caressed her bare skin and there was such reverence in his touch that Roxie's heart careened against her rib cage.

Slowly he eased one finger inside of her and her juice flowed warm and wet. He stroked the tip of his pinkie finger over her throbbing nib with just the barest hint of pressure and then gently slid back.

The velvety chafing, the considerate vigor, the excruciating rupture of awareness as his finger strummed her clit had Roxie's head spinning dizzily. She could not take it all. Her palms, splayed against the wall, were damp with sweet stress.

He stroked her harder, faster. Again and again. His focus was amazing, the way he was touching her made her feel cherished and cared for.

And that thought worried her almost as much as it pleased her.

Each firm but gentle stroke edged her closer to insanity. Then he placed a thumb at the entrance to her bottom, lightly rimmed the outside of her ass.

What was he doing?

"Do you like for me to touch you this way, my lady?"

Roxie nodded, held her breath. Her bottom was so achy, the feel of his thumb so exquisite.

"Tell me."

"I like it," she whispered.

He slid a third finger inside her feminine core, filling her up. His pinkie slid over her clit, his thumb rhythmically stroking outside her eager opening.

Sir Gareth increased the tempo. The fact that at any moment her father's henchmen could come up those stones steps and see him pressing his body against Lady Sarah's naked ass made her hornier than ever.

"More," she murmured. "More, more, more."

Through the material of his pants, she could feel his rock-hard penis. Realizing how much he wanted her made her want him all the more.

His hand played her. Fingers, thumbs, faster and faster.

Inside the sexy haze, in the electricity that was her own

skin, Lady Sarah squeezed her eyes closed and listened to the thumping piston that was her heart sending her blood rolling hot and thick through her veins.

His mischievous thumb edged into her. Pushing her to places she'd never been, giving her new roles to play, novel dreams to dream, fresh wings to fly.

Delight flooded her brain, pleasure blinded her, wanting lit up every cell in her body. She was lost, and she could not see or smell or hear or taste or touch.

But Sir Gareth offered the way out, his fingers giving her a joy beyond measure.

This sweet invasion was more than she could comprehend. The sensations were completely out of the realm of anything she had ever experienced. Lady Sarah was transported. Her pleasure was that intense, her passion that great.

She was gasping and crying and begging for more. She was tumbling, soaring, shuddering.

Who knew, who knew, who knew it could feel like this?

The muscles of her womb spasmed, squeezing tight, and Roxie experienced a release that transcended everything. The feeling sent her soaring, past time and place, through galaxies and universes. In great, writhing echoes of pleasure, she came and came and came.

ON THE WAY BACK TO THE RESORT, Dougal brooded. What the hell was wrong with him? He'd abandoned the tour group and just followed right after Roxie as if he didn't have a brain. What would have happened if someone had caught them?

The idea appalled him, but it was the very thing that had made their illicit hookup exciting.

Pervert.

He needed to get his head back on his job, remember the reason he was here and stop thinking about Roxie. But how could he do that when just the sight of her clouded his mind and narrowed his focus to his cock?

What had happened to his control? How had he let this thing between them turn into a full-blown sexcapade? He dared to dart a gaze to the back of the bus.

Roxie sat beside Jess and Sam, talking and laughing. Absentmindedly she reached up to tuck a strand of hair behind her ear.

Damn, how he wished she was stroking him.

He had never intended on following Roxie inside the old church, and his unmanageable impulses had him questioning his principles. He'd signed a morality clause. He was breaking all the rules. Yes, he hadn't completely crossed the line. They hadn't made love all the way yet, but damn nearly had. The lines had blurred, and he was losing all sense of right and wrong. If he kept going with this affair, he was risking losing himself, and that scared Dougal more than he cared to admit.

All the way back to the resort, his tangled mind gnawed on the dilemma. What should he do about Roxie? He didn't find any answers, and in fact, as she got off the bus and he caught a whiff of her sensual scent, he felt his control unraveling all over again.

Gerry met him as he walked into the lobby. "Canna speak with you a moment?"

"What's up?" Dougal asked, fearing that somehow Gerry had guessed his secret.

"Step into my office." Gerry led him down the corridor and when the door was closed behind them, he perched on the corner of his desk and said, "Somethin' else 'as occurred."

"What happened?"

"Someone beheaded the water sprinklers inna back garden," Gerry explained.

Okay, Dougal thought. Maybe this wasn't connected. Cutting off sprinkler heads wasn't in the same league as tampering with a plane or rigging a spotlight to fall. "When?"

"I don't know for certain. The sprinklers were workin' last night, but the gardeners discovered the problem this mornin' after you'd already left with the tour group. I thought about callin' or textin' ya, but it didn't seem that big an issue. We've already bought new sprinkler heads and they're bein' replaced. Do ya think it could be the same person who tampered with the spotlight?"

Dougal shook his head. "I don't know."

"It seems more like petty vandalism than sabotage. Maybe there's no connection."

And maybe there is.

"What about the security cameras?" Dougal asked.

"There's no camera inna back garden," Gerry said, "but I've footage of the side gardens and the back patio area."

"Have you reviewed them?"

"Ya."

"Anything alert your interest?"

"Not really. But a guest was out strollin' the gardens at 3 a.m."

"Can you cue up the tape for me?"

"Sure." Gerry went to his computer, typed on the keyboard and in a few moments camera surveillance of the side gardens popped into view. The gardens looked beautiful in the moonlight. After a couple of seconds a woman stepped from one of the cottages. She was too far away to make out her features, but then she came closer, moving over the cobblestone walkway through the flowers. She had her head down, sweater wrapped tightly around her.

Then she looked up and the camera caught her face.

Dougal's stomach tightened.

It was Roxie.

ROXIE'S BODY STILL BURNED from the encounter she'd had with Dougal in the bell tower. The achy throb between her legs a sweet reminder of what they'd done. She was wild with wanting and couldn't wait to have more delicious sexual adventures with him.

And from now on, she wasn't going anywhere without a condom.

She dug through the gift basket left in her cottage, pulling out all the prophylactics and stuffing them in her purse. There was a sucker in the basket in the shape of a penis. Feeling giddy at the erotic whimsy, she laughed and opened the sucker and stuck it in her mouth.

Mmm, cherry.

She was humming to herself and licking her lollipop when the doorbell rang. When she looked through the peephole and saw it was Dougal, she tossed her sucker in the trash and flung open the door.

"Hi," she greeted him.

"Hello," he said, his voice subdued, his eyes somber. "Can we talk?"

"Sure, sure." She stood aside and waved him in. "Would you like something to drink? Water? Soda? Wine? Or I could make a pot of coffee."

"Water's fine."

She took bottles of water from the well-stocked fridge and held one out to him. He sauntered closer, his masculinity assaulting her senses. Her breath caught and her chest rose, gently pulling against the nubby texture of her robe. His dark, enigmatic eyes snared hers and she felt time simultaneously contract and expand, creating a surreal sensation as if she'd stepped into the pages of a fairy-tale storybook.

Their fingers touched in the transfer of the water bottle. It was barely discernible, the gentle brushing of his skin against hers and yet she felt it shoot straight to the center of her stomach.

"Thanks." He smiled, revealing white teeth that contrasted

sexily with his tanned skin and the reddish highlights in his dark, well-trimmed beard, but his smile didn't reach his eyes.

"Let's sit down," he said.

"Okay."

He plunked down on the couch in the sitting area; Roxie perched on the chair opposite him.

"Um, so what was it you wanted to discuss?" she ventured.

He sat with his legs spread apart, his elbows resting on his knees, his hands—clasping the water bottle—dangling between his legs. He canted his head, met her gaze. "Is there anything that you want to tell me?"

A ripple of apprehension ran over her. "Um…no. Why do you ask?"

His eyes darkened. "Why did you really come on this tour alone?"

"Didn't I tell you? My date backed out on me at the last minute," she lied, and immediately wondered why she'd done so. Normally she was a very honest person. Had spying on Eros for her boss already started her sliding down a slippery slope of sin?

"You didn't consider canceling your trip?"

She raised her jaw. "Why should I?"

"A lot of other women would have."

"I'm not like a lot of other women."

"I can see that."

"I needed an adventure." That much was true. She hadn't had a good adventure since, well…*never.*

"So that was the only reason you came to England alone? No secret agenda?"

His question caused her pulse to race. Why was he asking her that? Could he suspect what she was really doing here? Had she somehow inadvertently given herself away? Darn it, she'd told her boss she was wrong for this job.

Dougal leaned in closer. Was it her imagination or was that a glint of something very sensual in his eyes? Was he—like she—thinking about what had happened in that bell tower?

He did not look away. She wanted to drop her gaze, but she was afraid that he'd read something into it if she did— like guilt. *Cool it. You're going to give yourself away.* "No other reason."

Damn! Her voice sounded too high, too reedy, too jumpy.

"Just looking for adventure, huh?" He leaned back against the couch.

"Yes." What was he hinting at? "What's this all about?"

"About today…" He paused, futzing with the label on his water bottle and not meeting her eye.

Omigosh, he was regretting it. Her cheeks flamed. Roxie gulped. "Yes?"

"I don't want you to take this the wrong way. You're great. Better than great. You're a really special woman. It's just that I—"

"I get it," she interrupted, struggling to tamp down the dismay rising inside her and the feeling that she'd been a silly fool. "I've given men the brush-off before. The old 'it's not you, it's me' routine. Seriously, Dougal, don't give it a second thought. I had fun, you had fun…" She shrugged like it was no big deal.

"It's that it's so intense and moving so fast…"

"It's bound to burn out just as quickly," she finished for him.

"So you feel the same way?" He looked so relieved she wanted to reach out and smack him.

"Hey," she said, feigning nonchalance, "I was up for a casual thing, but I understand your job prohibits it."

"I'm sorry," he apologized. "I shouldn't have done what I did. It was wrong. I led you on."

She crossed her arms over her chest. "You did."

"But this thing between you and me." He toggled his finger back and forth. "It simply can't go any further."

She gulped, nodded, even though she longed to ask, "Why not?"

"Will you accept my apology?"

What could she say? She forced a smile. "Of course, but there's no reason for you to apologize."

"Thank you, Roxie. You're one class act."

Yeah? Well, what was she supposed to do about this unpleasant feeling mucking around inside her?

"There's one other thing."

"Yes?"

"Maybe you should skip the tour for the next couple of days. Stay in Stratford, do some local sightseeing. Get a massage on the house. Hang out at the pool."

"You're kicking me off the tour?" Something inside her shriveled.

"No, no, it's just that if we gave this thing a couple of days to cool down, maybe it wouldn't be so difficult for either of us to resist temptation."

"Okay, sure, fine," she rushed to assure him. She didn't want Dougal Lockhart thinking she cared.

He stood up and held out his hand, the same hand that had done very intimate things to her just hours before. "Friends?"

She took his hand, shook it and lied. "Friends."

LEAVING HER COTTAGE feeling worse than when he'd arrived, Dougal went to his own living quarters. His plan had backfired. He'd gone to coax a confession out of Roxie, and instead he'd felt such overwhelming chemistry it had been all he could do to get out of there without ripping her clothes off and doing her on the rug, carpet burns be damned.

He'd sat and looked at her and realized there was no way

she could have decapitated those sprinkler heads or tampered with the spotlights or messed with the autopilot on the airplane. At least that's what his gut was telling him.

But his mind—his cautious, distrustful mind—was telling him he could not completely ignore the fact that Roxie had been in the gardens around the time the sprinklers had been vandalized. Plus, who was she really? She could have the technological know-how to sabotage the autopilot. Or she could be working with a skilled accomplice. It was flimsy evidence at best, and the only concrete thing he had to link her to any of the problems at the resort. By focusing on her, he was closing himself off to other possible suspects.

His head wasn't in the game. His brain was lust-glazed, his body consumed. He'd had to break the spell she'd woven over him and telling her that they could not take their relationship any further was a step in that direction. And he'd lied about being friends. There was no way he could just be friends with her.

It had been a painful moment, but he'd made the right call. Besides, if she stayed behind at the resort for the next few days and something else happened, his doubts about her innocence would be solidified. Conversely, if nothing happened, it would go a long way in proving that his gut was right, that she wasn't involved in any kind of subterfuge.

Unless, whispered the doubting voice at the back of his head, *she's smart enough not to make a move when most of the other guests are away from the resort.*

Roxie's not like that, argued his stubborn gut. She was honest and genuine and open-minded. She didn't seem furtive at all.

Except Dougal no longer knew if this was his gut that was talking. It could easily be his penis.

Or even worse…*his heart.*

9

FOR THE NEXT FOUR DAYS, Roxie stayed at the resort. In
between the spying and researching she did for Porter Langley,
collecting a lot of information about the inner workings of
Eros, taking photos, talking to employees and e-mailing
updates to her boss, she did as Dougal suggested. She visited
the Eros spa, got a manicure and a pedicure, a facial and a two-
hour massage. She had to admit that after years of self-
sacrifice and denial, it felt luxuriously decadent to pamper
herself. But even as she did so, she couldn't help feeling guilty
for what she was doing. Not because it was illegal, but because
it went against her moral code. She felt as if she was betraying
Dougal—having a good time at his resort and essentially
stabbing him in the back at the same time.

She tried to forget everything by renting an inner tube and
spending one whole day just floating around in the heated
moat. Another day she walked into Stratford and took a self-
guided tour of the town. Then on Friday, she went shopping,
buying souvenirs for Stacy and her friends. That same afternoon, she'd explored the grounds of the castle and she discovered a replica of a medieval torture chamber in the dungeon that
she found both exciting and disturbing. But no matter what she
was doing or what she found to occupy herself, Dougal was
never far from her mind.

Constant fantasies bombarded her and more than once, she

took respite in the bathtub, filling it with hot water and scented bath beads, leaning back against the cool porcelain and rubbing herself in all the right places with a nubby washrag. It had given her some physical relief, but her mental torture kept building. Why on earth couldn't she stop thinking about that man?

It's because he never finished what he started, she rationalized.

On Saturday, Eros was throwing a Lord Byron-themed Regency ball. The slogan was Mad, Bad and Dangerous to Know, the reigning color scheme lavender and gold. Guests were encouraged to dress in the garb of their favorite Regency-era character and wear provocative masks. Roxie was excited about attending and seeing Dougal again. It would be interesting to learn if time apart had dampened their enthusiasm for each other or whetted it.

Roxie dressed in a floor-length gown, which according to the lady at the checkout kiosk of the costume room was exactly like something Jane Austen would have worn to a party of this caliber. "You'll be the spitting image of Elizabeth Bennet," the woman had assured her. Roxie had also picked out a purple sequined mask that matched the violet wood sorrels on the print of her dress. When she put it on, she had to admit she felt utterly bewitched.

Guests packed the ballroom dressed as Jane Austen, Beau Brummell, the first Duke of Wellington, Lady Caroline Lamb, Princess Lieven, Walter Scott, William Wordsworth and many other colorful historical figures. There were also dozens of Elizabeth Bennets and Mr. Darcys, but that was to be expected.

Roxie made note of the attention to detail Taylor Corben lavished on the event. From the romantic decor to the lyrical music to the lavish buffet, everything was impeccable. The romantic atmosphere swept everyone back in time to that manners-driven era sandwiched between the Georgian and Victorian periods. Darn if she didn't feel as though she'd stepped into an 1813 drawing room.

She arrived at the party at the same time Sam and Jess did, but immediately after entering the grand ballroom, her gaze skimmed over the gathering. After several minutes, she thought she spied Dougal in the corner with his back to her talking to one of the staff members, but then he turned, and the man was beardless. Still, how many men possessed shoulders like his?

He looked up and from behind his exotic black mask, his eyes met hers and she had no more doubts. It was Dougal after all, looking for all the world like Mr. Darcy himself in his period attire.

Her heart tripped.

She missed the skintight leather *Shakespeare in Love* pants, but he did look just as fine in riding breeches and his clean-shaven jaw. The sight of his unadorned face took her breath away. His chin was firmer, larger than she'd imagined. The difference in his appearance heightened her awareness.

And her arousal.

He stalked across the ballroom toward her.

Fear and longing did a tandem tango through Roxie's body, pounding her heart, bubbling her blood, setting little firestorms up and down her nerve endings. Her muscles tensed and her knees weakened.

"Hi," he said, drawing near.

"Hi," she answered, sounding all girlish and breathy.

Even in the Regency finery, everything about him was rugged, all male. He had the kind of masculinity that couldn't be defined by clothing or facial hair. His nails were clipped short, but not manicured. His palms were calloused. Old scars crisscrossed the back of his knuckles as if he'd had to punch his way out of more than a few arguments. He had a flinty-eyed, old-fashioned-movie-lawman aura about him beneath the Mr. Darcy facade.

She didn't know what to say to him after not having spoken

to him for four days, so she just gave him a coy smile and ducked her head.

"Would you like to dance?" he asked.

"Wouldn't that be breaking the rules?"

"It's a party. I'm expected to mingle with the guests."

"Ah, so that's it."

"You're going to make me beg, aren't you?" He smiled.

"You did dump me."

"Alas, to my regret."

"Are you admitting it was a mistake?" She could not stop a thrill of excitement from zipping through her.

"I am." He bowed, held out his hand. "Pray, Miss Bennet, a dance?"

Oh, he'd already figured out her weakness. The bastard.

"I do not know this dance."

"I shall teach you."

"Pray, dear sir, do you honestly wish to suffer trampled toes?"

"My toes are my own concern, dear lady. I suspect your hesitation has less to do with your dancing skills and more to do with your fear of my proximity."

"You are goading me, sir."

"A challenge perhaps, but goading, no."

"Since you have issued a challenge, it appears I am not in a position to deny you this dance."

"Indeed." He raised a rakish eyebrow that jutted up high above his mask and proffered his hand.

How could she resist? Roxie smiled and placed her hand in his.

She was a little nervous about dancing, but the minute he winked reassuringly, she felt more at ease. Have fun. Live in the moment. Tonight would make up for all the things she'd missed—senior prom and the homecoming game, the senior class trip, her graduation ceremony, having a boyfriend in high school.

Dougal, it seemed, was fully in command of the dance floor.

She simply followed his lead, letting him take charge. Oddly enough there was something highly erotic about the simple contact of their hands in the midst of the communal line dance. The music was bouncy and lively, and she quickly found herself laughing breathlessly with the rest of the group.

Who knew dancing could be so much fun? More accurately, who knew dancing with Dougal could be this much fun? She was enjoying herself more than she ever had, but she didn't feel the least bit guilty about it.

The song ended and they broke apart. A sheen of perspiration dampened her brow, and she wiped it away with the back of her hand. "Mr. Darcy," she said. "You have certainly proven your dancing skills. You may extend my compliments to your mother for insisting you learn the proper way to propel a young lady across the dance floor."

"My mother will be quite pleased to hear of your compliment," he said. "And might I add I appreciate that you did not once trample upon my toes."

"You are most welcome, Mr. Darcy."

"May I offer you some refreshment after our exertion? Some water perhaps? Or would a stronger beverage be to your liking?"

"Water is in order." She fanned herself with a hand. "Thank you kindly for your offer."

It wasn't so much the dancing that overheated her but staring at Dougal, who didn't seem the least bit winded. The man was amazing—virile, strong, loaded with stamina. Most of the guys she'd gone out with were cerebral, long on college degrees, short on actual real-world experiences. They loved to pontificate and get into intellectual discussions, but when it came to putting theory into action they moved with the speed of a stone pony. Sudden insight dawned. Was dating professor types her way of rubbing elbows with the education she'd never received?

She pondered this realization and it made her look at Dougal in a whole new light. He wasn't her usual type and yet he made her feel more alive than any man she'd ever been with. Was he the perfect antidote she needed to shake her from this habit of choosing men who seemed to make up for what she lacked? Being with him jolted her system. He was a worldly man, who'd really lived. Not a pontificating professor who'd spent his life wrapped up in books.

He escorted her to the bar, where he requested two glasses of water, then headed for an empty table in the corner. She followed, trailing awkwardness behind her. Once they were off the dance floor, she had time to realize that hanging out with him was counterproductive to her mission as a corporate spy, but she couldn't seem to help herself.

All the more reason to tell him good-night.

He set down their drinks and then pulled out a chair for her. His mother had clearly raised a gentleman. Roxie sat and he stopped to unbutton the jacket of his costume.

"It is growing quite warm in the confines of the building," he explained.

You can say that again. She felt a trickle of sweat slide between her breasts.

"Would you find me too forward if I removed my outer garment?"

"By all means, Mr. Darcy. Your comfort is my utmost concern."

"I appreciate your permission to cool myself." He stripped the jacket off his shoulders and draped it over the back of his chair. Roxie couldn't stop herself from watching his small striptease.

Looking more obscenely impressive than Lord Byron himself, Dougal scooted his chair as close to hers as he could get and sat. She shut her eyes and bit down on her bottom lip, willing herself not to be so aware of him, but it was futile.

He was so near she could smell him. His scent, a pleasing,

masculine aroma—part soap, part perspiration, part spray-starch, part leather—crept over her. If it was a color it would be verdant Kelly green, live, rich and fertile.

Dougal shifted in his seat; his thigh briefly brushed against hers. Accidental or intentional? His eyes behind that dark mask were enigmatic.

Did it matter? The touch immediately caused her thigh to tingle. Nervously she drummed her fingernails against the tabletop.

Dougal closed his hand over hers, stopping her restless tapping. She waited for him to say something, but he did not. He just held her hand.

Roxie forgot to breathe, and she didn't dare raise her gaze to meet his. She didn't know what else to do so she simply sat there, sipping her water, staring at the dancers, aware of nothing but the pressure of his hand on hers.

"Would you like to discuss what is troubling you?" he asked after a very long moment.

"I have no need to offer conversation," she said, her words tumbling out on a whoosh of pent-up air. She was in over her head with this guy, like an inexperienced swimmer who'd wandered away from the kiddie pool and found herself in deep water with no life preserver in sight. Time apart served to sharpen her awareness of him, not thwart it as she'd hoped.

"You seem quite agitated, my dear Miss Bennet."

Roxie blew out her breath on a flippant puff of denial. "No, not I, sir. Agitated is not a state of mind with which I am familiar."

"Pray tell, then, why does your knee bob up and down so vigorously?"

Was she doing that? Lovely, she was. She placed her free hand on her knee to stop her fidgeting. "I fear I have developed an annoying habit," she explained.

"Might a case of nerves be the reason behind this nervous habit of yours?" he asked.

"Absolutely not, sir. I have no call to be nervous about anything."

"No?" There went that eyebrow again, launching higher on his forehead.

"No." That was her story and she was sticking to it. She raised her hand to nibble on her thumbnail but stopped herself with her hand halfway to her mouth, grimacing at her action.

"Ah." He cracked a smile but his tone said he wasn't buying her explanation, not for a second. "I thought maybe I'd flustered you."

"Not at all." Okay, where did she sign up for the liar's hall of shame? She was a shoo-in.

He held fast to her hand.

Roxie ached to snatch her hand away, but she couldn't because then it would confirm she was a great big fibber and he *had* flustered her. "You know," she said, "everyone has nervous habits."

Dougal said nothing, but stared at her through half-lowered lids, the look in his eyes weighted with hidden meaning.

She reached out to trace her fingertips over his clean-shaven jaw. She felt the muscle tense beneath her touch even as she saw he was steeling himself not to flinch. What was she doing?

"Now who's flustered?" she whispered, amazed at how she'd managed to turn the tables on him and thrilled at her brazenness.

He interlaced his fingers through hers, holding her hand anchored to the table. No escape. It was as if he was waiting for her to tell him the truth, spill her guts about why she was really here.

She thought of the first time she'd seen the movie *Bambi* when she was six years old. The most vivid scene for her had been the one where two quails were hunkered down in the grass, trying to be quiet to avoid a gun-toting hunter stalking closer and closer and closer. Watching it, she'd known that if the quails just didn't make a move, if they would just stay cool, their lives would be spared. But the tension tightened with each encroaching footstep. Then the hunter had suddenly stopped oh so near those crouching birds. Roxie remembered holding her breath at that point in the movie, her stomach twisted into knots, her fist clenched. Finally one of the quails screamed, "I can't take it anymore," flew into the air, revealing herself to the hunter, and he shot her dead.

Right now she felt exactly like that panicky quail, and Dougal was shooting her dead with his glittery dark eyes. He tightened his fingers around hers.

Stay quiet. Reveal nothing. Don't lose it and expose yourself.

His eyes burned into hers, his gaze stealing all the oxygen from the room.

"I do have a sinful secret," she whispered.

Don't be a quail.

Dougal's mouth opened slightly. His lips were full and sensuous, the skin of his chin smooth where he'd shaved. His chest jerked up and then inward with each compelling breath. His scent, that devastating scent of his, assailed her nostrils.

"What is it?" he murmured. He was positioned between her and the door. Getting away from him wasn't a viable option. She had to deal with this to the end. What would Mata Hari do?

For years, Roxie had suppressed her impulses, placing Stacy's needs above her own. She'd done it for so long, second-guessing herself was default mode. But the panicky sensation that quail had experienced swept over her and she simply reacted.

She got up, crooked a finger at him. "Come with me, Mr. Darcy."

HE SHOULDN'T FOLLOW HER. Dougal knew it, and yet when it came to Roxie, he possessed zero self-control. Add to that the fact that he hadn't seen her in four days and he was off-the-charts horny.

Where was she leading him?

It didn't really matter for it seemed he would go with her to the ends of the earth if that's where she took him.

Four days without her had been pure torture, and when there had been no further incidents of sabotage in that time, his gut told him she was innocent, even as his mind told him he was a fool for letting down his guard.

She moved through the crowd of masked partygoers and out the side exit, his attention fixed on her swaying hips. God, how he loved her curvy feminine figure. He was just itching to cup her round, full bottom in the palms of his hands.

"Where are we going?" he asked.

She didn't answer him, just kept walking, and her silence only served to escalate his desire. She wandered down the corridors, her shoes echoing against the stone. He was getting so hard he was having trouble walking.

She descended a long flight of stairs. Down, down, down they went.

At the bottom of the stairs was a stone door. She stopped, turned her head and glanced at him over her shoulder. Her blue eyes looked deliciously cool beneath her purple sequined mask. She put out her sweet pink tongue and swept it across her lips. His heart galloped.

Still, she did not speak. She pushed open the heavy door. It swung inward with a groan revealing a dark, narrow foyer lit only by flickering wall sconces. Excitement pressed tight against his chest.

She stepped over the threshold and he followed.

Once inside, the door automatically creaked closed behind them. They were in a dungeon.

"I have a feeling we're no longer Elizabeth Bennet and Mr. Darcy." He chuckled nervously.

She reached for something on the wall. He didn't see what it was, but he heard the unmistakable crack of a whip. Instantly his balls drew up tight against his body. "Into the chamber with you, heretic," she roared.

Trepidation raised the hairs on his arms, and Dougal realized he'd never in his life been so turned on.

Another door creaked—metal, this time, from the sound of it—and another faint glow of flickering orange light. A cool draft blew across his face. It smelled musky and damp like sex. She cracked the whip again. "Inside!"

He went.

She slammed the door behind them and turned a big black skeleton key in the lock.

The stone walls had iron manacles mounted on them. Dougal gulped. Oh shit, he thought and his cock got so hard he feared he might shoot his wad then and there.

"Stand here." She flicked the whip at the spot on the floor beneath the manacles.

Compelled by a force he could not explain or manage, he obeyed.

Her role-playing was exciting. She could slip under the skin of anyone and fully become that character. She was everything he was not. She was expressive, unrestrained, eager. She was real and true with her sexuality, and he admired her for it.

"Arms up."

He raised his arms over his head.

She had to reach up to clamp the manacles around his wrists and when she did, her breasts grazed his chest, and he groaned at the contact. The woman was driving him insane.

Roxie slid to her knees in front of him, and then coyly canted her head up. A wild glow of excitement sparked in those eyes behind that mask. The contour of her lips changed, her posture was looser. Her fingers worked frantically, undoing his pants. She tugged his trousers and underwear to his ankles, revealing his jutting, rock-hard cock.

He flinched at the first touch of her mouth on him, but her lips felt so hot and wet around his shaft that Dougal couldn't help groaning. The sensation was achingly sweet and so powerful he was grateful for the manacles that kept him from toppling over.

He was a lucky, lucky bastard. No doubt about it. He looked down at her and his heart stuttered. He swayed.

She spread her hands over his buttocks to help steady him, her fingers splaying into him. And when her mouth latched on to him with a strong suction, Dougal's eyes rolled back in his head. She was lapping and suckling as if she could never get enough of him. He knew he couldn't get enough of her.

She tickled the small of his back with one hand, cupped his balls with the other. Dougal almost yelped. It felt damned incredible.

Systematically she set about dismantling him with her mouth.

He felt embarrassed then, and in spite of his body's intense ache, he wanted to break free from the manacles, reach down to pull her to her feet, but he was ensnared in a chaotic whirl-wind of sensation. He was afraid. He wanted his control back. He wanted to feel balanced again. This powerful sexual attrac-tion caused him an inner discord that went against his nature.

Dougal moaned as the heat escalated inside him. Her rhythm picked up. Her hands slid all over his body. Inde-scribable, this intimacy. His chest expanded, tightened. It was unlike anything he'd ever experienced. This took the meaning of sex to a whole new level.

"Yes," he hissed as she moved back and forth. "Yes, yes, yes."

Roxie worked her magic with her fingers, her tongue leading him into uncharted territory. He was on sensory overload as she gently guided him to a paradise he'd only dreamed of.

But this wasn't a dream. The warm wetness of her mouth on his cock, the heavenly smell of her femininity, the greedy sound of her tongue swirled through him. This new awareness of her was breaking up his brittle outer shell.

She was beyond beauty to him. She was pure life, pure joy. She and her sensual impulses merged together against all the rules of proper conduct. Her mouth moved over him without caution or fear. She pushed him past his knowledge of himself. He had never before been so physically possessed. The dungeon walls seemed to ripple. Could this be an earthquake?

No. The ground did not tremble, only his body. Dougal was nervous and exalted and awed. He accepted the inevitable.

"Yes," she murmured. "That's right. Let go. Give up everything."

How had she discerned the mental shift in him? The letting go?

Relentlessly, Roxie pushed him forward. He was aching, gushing, throbbing, beating. He threw back his head and cried out, pleading for release from this magnificent torture, from the ecstasy he could almost touch.

Soon. Please, please let it be soon. It had better be or he was going to drop dead from need.

And then, just like that, it was upon him.

Dougal tumbled. Jerking and trembling into the abyss, the world cracked open, enveloped him.

He peered down, blinked. He could barely see. Roxie was sitting at his feet, smiling coyly, her lips glistening creamy and wet. She winked at him and then sweetly swallowed his essence.

If he hadn't been manacled, Dougal would have pitched

forward onto his knees. Instead, he hung there sweating, shuddering, panting for breath.

He was used up, spent. His cock emptied as he struggled to wrap his mind around what had just happened.

10

ON SUNDAY MORNING, the bus took them for a day trip to Cambridge. The schedule was unstructured, allowing guests to choose from a variety of activities. There was shopping in Market Square and King's Parade, tours of the local colleges and museums, helicopter tours for hire or punting on the Cambridge River. A punt was a flat-bottomed boat with a square bow, used to navigate shallow bodies of water. Roxie, Jess and Sam elected to try their hand at maneuvering these unwieldy watercrafts.

"What are you doing for the day?" Jess quizzed Dougal as they got off the bus.

"I'm going to hang out at the commons." He didn't look at Roxie nor she at him. Not for one second had he been able to stop thinking about what had happened in the dungeon last night.

"Have you ever punted before?" Sam asked.

"I have," Dougal admitted.

"Where did you learn how to punt?" Roxie asked.

"I was in the Air Force, remember?" Dougal smiled. "I was stationed at Lakenheath, which is only twenty-five miles from here. My friends and I frequently came down to punt the Cam when we were on leave."

"Then come hang out with us," Sam said. "We're going to buy a picnic lunch and take the river to Grantchester. I've even brought a blanket for picnicking." She held up the thin cotton blanket she had tucked under her arm.

"That's a long way. Perhaps you should just punt The Backs. It's only takes thirty minutes. Grantchester and back is a four-hour round-trip."

"We've got friends who went to college here and they said everyone does The Backs," Jess said, referring to the waterway that ran behind the row of colleges. "We want something lazier, less crowded and more relaxed."

"Have you ever punted before?" Dougal asked.

"No." Jess grinned. "Why do you think we're inviting you along?"

"You could hire a chauffeured punt," he pointed out.

"But we like you."

"You want me to take you to Grantchester?" Dougal slid Roxie a quick glance. She shrugged. She had no idea Jess was going to ask him along for the ride.

"Pretty please?" Jess clasped her hands together as if she was saying a prayer.

"That wouldn't be fair to the other guests," Roxie said, giving him an out. "I'm sure they'd all like Dougal to punt them on the Cam."

"Yes," Jess said, "but I asked, and they didn't."

Dougal laughed.

"We tip big," Sam added.

Dougal looked straight at Roxie. "How can I say no with such beautiful enticements?"

"Oh, goodie." Jesse danced a little jig. "Let's go."

Thirty minutes later, they were on their way in the small, flat-bottomed boat. It was long and thin and rectangular in shape with just enough room to seat two people next to each other. This particular punt was designed to carry five—two couples inside the boat, the punter out on the platform at the stern. Jess and Sam wedged in together, a big picnic basket at their feet.

Roxie sat alone, closest to the platform where Dougal stood, holding a long, thick pole.

They scooted under a bridge, headed away from the majority of the punters angling for The Backs. The weather was gorgeous—blue skies with soft puffs of clouds, mild temperature, a soft caressing breeze. And the view from the river! The architecture of the old buildings stirred the imagination as did the beautiful gardens. Ducks floated by looking for handouts from the boaters.

In the distance, church bells rang, announcing the 10 a.m. hour. It didn't take long until they'd left most of the buildings behind and found themselves surrounded by lush green fields on both sides of the river.

Jess and Sam chattered all the way to Grantchester. Roxie tried to pay attention, but Dougal's proximity derailed her focus. He handled the punt like a pro, and she couldn't stop herself from watching him. His movements were smooth, muscles rippling underneath the sleeves of his shirt. Because he wasn't guiding a tour today, he wasn't in costume and wore blue jeans and a blue polo shirt with a collar, and he'd traded his boots for sneakers.

Dressed in street clothes, he looked like a different person, and she found herself loving this new image of him. It was a cleaner look, simple and direct. Was this the real Dougal? she wondered.

They were halfway to Grantchester when a punt passed by them, headed toward Cambridge with two young men aboard. "Jess? Sam? Is that you?" one of them asked.

"David! Mike!" Jess and Sam squealed simultaneously and waved at their friends.

It turned out that Jess and Sam had gone to college with David and Mike, who were backpacking their way through Europe. The punts stopped side by side for some conversation. David and Mike were leaving Cambridge later that day, and they bemoaned the fact they wouldn't get to see more of Jess and Sam.

"We could go back with you," Sam said, shifting her gaze to Dougal. "If that's okay with you and Roxie."

Dougal shrugged. "It's your vacation. Just remember the bus back to Stratford leaves at six."

"What about the picnic?" Roxie asked.

"We'll feed you girls," David spoke up. "A late lunch at Whims?"

"That's the best restaurant in Cambridge," Jess exclaimed. "I'm in."

"You and Dougal can keep the picnic basket," Sam added.

Then Jess and Sam carefully transferred over into David and Mike's punt and the group poled away.

"What are you grinning about?" Dougal asked Roxie when their friends had disappeared from sight.

"We're all alone."

His eyes twinkled. "That we are. Would you like to learn how to punt?"

"Another adventure," she said. "Sure."

He laughed.

"What?"

"You're like a kid. So bright-eyed and eager."

"Hey, I spent a long time not having adventures. I'm not going to pass up a single one."

"Then come up here and take hold of the pole. But first let's review the golden rule of punting."

"Which is?"

"Stay with the punt, not the pole."

He got down from the platform and held out his hand to help her up, then he passed her the pole. She eyed the platform suspiciously. It looked scary, slippery and not very big. Tentatively she took her position and the ridiculously long ten-foot pole, acutely aware of her wavering balance.

Nervously she glanced over at Dougal who'd sat down in the boat. "What do I do now?"

"Hold the pole upright and over the right-hand side of the punt, drop the pole into the water and position it slightly behind where you're standing. If the pole is too far away from the punt, it will go in circles when you push. If you put the pole in the water level to or ahead of you, the punt will go backward," he explained.

She did as he suggested and felt the pole land solidly on the bottom.

"Now push down on the pole. The harder you push, the faster you'll go."

Roxie pushed and the punt glided forward, but the pole wouldn't budge from the mud. "What do I do?"

"Let go of the pole!" Dougal said, but his warning came too late. The punt was out from under her and she was holding on to the pole in the middle of the water.

"Help!" she managed just as the pole starting leaning over against her weight. She was going in, no two ways about it.

But then suddenly, there was Dougal, paddle in hand, angling the punt right back to her and she was able to get one foot back on the platform and right herself with only one leg getting wet.

"You saved my fanny," she said.

"You forgot the golden rule." Dougal chuckled. "Don't worry. Everyone does their first time."

"I think maybe I've had enough of punting." She giggled. "You make it look so easy."

"No, go on, give it another go."

She took another stab at it, and this time she managed to propel the boat down the river without mishap. After a few more rounds of drop and push, she started to get the feel for it. The activity was more strenuous than she'd counted on.

"I'm getting tired," she said after several more minutes. "Could you take over?"

"How about we stop for lunch?"

"We're not at Grantchester."

"No law saying we have to go all the way. We can stop here." He waved at an inviting field. "Let's have lunch, and then punt on back to Cambridge."

"I'm for that," she agreed.

Dougal took over and angled them toward the riverbank. He tied up the punt, and then helped her ashore.

Roxie spread Jess's blanket beside a large weeping willow, making a nest among the brightly colored wildflowers sprinkled across the lush green grass. Out here in nature, with no one else around, it felt as though they were the only two people on their planet.

Dougal flopped down on the blanket beside her as she opened the white wicker picnic basket, his fingertips stroking her forearm so softly that at first she thought she was imagining it. Then she felt the tickle of his lips, hot and sexy, kissing a path up her arm. She glanced over at him, his eyes were half-closed, a lazy smile curled at the corners of his mouth. She loved the feel of his hard body beside hers.

"You look so relaxed," she said.

"Punting the Cam agrees with me."

"Me, too."

"What's in the basket?" He propped himself on his elbows.

"Let's see." Roxie lifted the blue gingham napkins and poked around inside. "Ah, a bottle of French wine. Sauvignon blanc. Two glasses and a corkscrew."

"Good start."

Roxie dug around in the basket. "Gourmet sandwiches. Hmm, let's see." She lifted the corner of the bread. "Yum, looks like roasted turkey and white cheddar with some kind of fancy fruit chutney on a baguette and a side dish of pearl couscous salad, plus apples and a variety of cheeses and oh my...*look*." She held up dessert for him to see.

Dougal broke into a grin. "Walnut brownies."

They ate in companionable silence, enjoying the beauty of the moment, savoring the delicious food, reveling in the company. Roxie's mind traveled, as it always did, to another time and place. They were indeed Adam and Eve, munching sinfully on apples and happily touching each other.

"Who are we now?" Dougal asked.

"What do you mean?"

"I know you enjoy playacting," he said. "The first day we were Shakespeare and his Muse. Then in the church we were star-crossed Sir Gareth and Lady Sarah. Last night we were Mr. Darcy and Elizabeth Bennet, before we turned into the dungeon dominatrix and torture victim." He grinned and her heart pumped with excitement as she remembered last night's sexual adventure. "Who are we today?"

"Adam and Eve," she admitted.

He looked around at the pastoral setting, and then his gaze tracked hotly over her body. "I can get into that."

Roxie's pulse quickened. She had never role-played with any of her other boyfriends and she was loving this.

"Let's see," he said. "You've just tempted me with your apple and as a matter of course, we must now sin." He took the apple core from her hand, tossed it aside.

She studied his face.

He looked at her as if he'd just tumbled out of bed, his hair wild and whorled, his eyes heavy-lidded and filled with the vestiges of a fantastic wet dream. She appreciated his body, dressed casually in that blue shirt and jeans. He looked rock-solid, substantial, an athlete with muscular legs and a strong back. And when he turned his head, she could see his muscles in one long ripple underneath his shirt.

Her hands tingled, yearning for his touch. Between her legs, she ached for him. The scent of fertile rich soil was potent and loamy, the smell kicking her arousal up a notch.

Dougal's eyes held hers and she knew he smelled it, too, their lust, brewing. She tasted him before their lips touched completely.

He reached out and took her hand and pulled her close, running his fingers along the curve of her back. He kissed her in the verdant green field dotted with beautiful wildflowers. The sweet smell of bluebells and forget-me-nots and musk mallow and meadow cranesbill mingled with the musky aroma of the water. Dougal was like that river. Strong and steady and reliable and Roxie couldn't resist. There was no point in even trying.

Dougal Lockhart was her downfall.

He lay on his back, and she stretched out on top of him, staring down at him, her thighs on either side of his waist.

He kissed her tenderly, tentative and questioning, as though he feared she might disappear if he was too bold. But how could he fear that after last night?

The breeze gusted and the willow tree branches rustled, blowing a wave of fluttering caresses over their skin. She touched her forehead to his, looking deep into his eyes, and her pulse shifted from a saunter to a trot.

Silence stretched heated and heavy. Something new was being created between them. Vistas as yet unexplored. She realized that her hands were trembling.

The blue vein at his temple throbbed. The tempo of its beat matched perfectly the aching in her sex.

Dougal kissed her again, deeper. He groaned and she felt the vibration of it rumble from his chest and the almost painful tightening of his hands around her waist.

She wanted him desperately. She had to get his clothes off him. Right this minute. She snatched at his shirt and he helped her wrestle it over his head. His skin was molten.

"Wait, wait, time-out," she said, suddenly realizing she didn't want to be in the same predicament she'd found herself in before, and pulled a condom from her bag.

He reached for the buttons of her dress and slowly began undoing them. With each button he loosened, her breathing sped up. After he undid the last button, he ran his hands under her camisole, pushing it aside so he could stroke her bare breasts.

Goose bumps spread over her skin, engulfing her in shivers. She was exposed, astride him in a pasture in broad daylight. It was a dulcet, decadent sensation. Roxie could feel exactly how hard he was for her.

"You are so beautiful," he said huskily. "The way the sun glints off your ebony hair. You take my breath away."

Dougal smelled like cotton and leather. He made her feel safe and taken care of when she hadn't really felt that way since her parents had been killed. It was a startling, disconcerting feeling. Roxie was used to being the protector, not the one being protected.

She closed her eyes, but she could still see the ocean of wildflowers waving merrily all around them. He was pinching her nipples gently but firmly, sending little rockets of pleasure flying across her nerve endings.

He sat up with her legs still positioned on either side of him and laved his tongue over one of her nipples while his hand stole down and slipped between her legs.

He was doing all the right things, touching her in all the right ways, giving her all the right looks. Misery crawled through her. She couldn't go through with it. Making love—really making love—with him wasn't fair to either one of them. Not when she was hiding her true identity.

"Dougal." It was a plea. "We need to talk."

"No talking. Not now. Just feel, Roxie."

How easy it was to just give in to the sensations sweeping through her. To relinquish all control as he eased her legs farther apart and planted a kiss on her knee.

Arching her spine, she rocked back a little on his pelvis, giving him freer entry. His hand slid down her belly, past the waistband of her panties. His fingertips found her clit and she gasped at the heat of his touch.

And then he started rocking against her, rhythmic and pleasing.

Her legs shook and she could feel the pressure of his body underneath her buttocks, pressing stiffly against her. He was panting, and she was panting until she didn't think she could bear one more minute of this torture.

In the distance they heard voices out on the river, another punt gliding along.

Someone was going to see them!

Frantically she tried to break away, to pull her dress closed around her nakedness, but Dougal wrapped one hand tight around her waist while at the same time pushing a finger deep inside of her. Sucking in her breath, she let out a cry of happy surprise as a hot wave of bliss passed over her.

He sat all the way up, pushing her down on her back. Her nose filled anew with the fertile smell of wildflowers and Dougal. He smiled down at her, his eyes mischievous. She could hear the people on the river laughing and joking.

"They're not going to stop," he said. "And neither am I."

Her heart clutched. She loved this dangerous game he was playing.

The sound of the people in the punt came closer, escalating her excitement. She moved, shifting away from him and went for his zipper, wanting his cock more than she'd ever wanted anything in her life.

Soon they were both completely naked, relishing in the glory of each other's bodies on the banks of the river Cambridge, far away from reality. They were Adam and Eve. New lovers, excited, giggling and exploring.

They stared into each other's eyes and smiled, embarrassed suddenly but in a good way. Roxie reached out to touch his face and he let her caress his clean-shaven chin, his mouth, his chest, but he closed his eyes. Did not look at her again.

Was he nervous? Or was he savoring this moment as much as she was?

"Have you ever done anything you deeply regretted?" he asked hoarsely.

"Haven't we all?" she whispered.

"Tell me, Roxie, what do you regret?"

"I regret not meeting you sooner," she said. "Look at all the fun I've been missing. What about you? Are you regretting this?"

"No." He squeezed her tightly. "Never."

"Not even putting your job on the line?"

"I wish I didn't have a morality clause in my contract because I'm not the kind of guy who goes back on his word, but when I'm around you I can't help myself. I have zero control." He kissed her again. "You do strange things to me, woman. You make me do things I wouldn't normally do."

"Right back at you, big man."

"Is that a bad thing or good?"

"You tell me," she whispered.

He finally opened his eyes and looked deeply into hers. "These last few days with you…"

"Yes?" She held her breath.

"They've been special." She could tell by his serious expression he did not say such things lightly. "You're special."

"I think you're special, too."

"But you scare me," he admitted. He looked so vulnerable in that moment, so utterly breakable.

"How so?"

"You have this wide-eyed innocence about you as if you've been sheltered most of your life, and yet you've also got this sensible, grounded side, as well. You're a bit of a paradox."

"Yeah, well, you're all rough and tough and manly and yet you're squiring tourists around Europe. Not that there's anything wrong with that, it's just not very…" She searched for the right word to describe him. "Urgent. You seem like the kind of guy who needs something urgent to do."

He looked at her with quizzical eyes and something else, an emotion she couldn't label. It was almost a sad expression, but not quite. It was more rueful. Or could it be disappointment?

Had she disappointed him in some way or did he fear that she would? "You've been hurt before."

"I have."

She fingered his lips. "You're not a man who easily gives his heart."

"I'm not," he whispered.

Now she was feeling as vulnerable as he looked. "If you're not ready, it's okay. This doesn't have to mean anything, Dougal. I'm not expecting anything from you." At least that's what she kept telling herself. "And I don't think you should expect anything from me other than what we've got in this moment, right now. Sex is enough."

"Roxie." He said her name on a sigh. "I want you, need you. Now."

She slipped her fingers through his hair, held his head still and kissed him with all the fervent intensity she had inside her. She was slick for him and he was hard for her.

His penis was so big, so awesome. She licked her lips. "Condom," she gasped. "Where's the condom?"

He found it.

…eration to have him, she snatched the condom

from his hand, ripped it open with her teeth and with trembling fingers, pushed him back just long enough to roll it on.

He pushed inside of her on a rush of heat. Her muscles tensed around him, drawing him in deeper.

"You are so tight." He groaned.

She couldn't answer. Emotion constricted her throat. She'd always dreamed of sex like this—wild and hungry and brilliantly good—but this was so much more than she'd ever bargained for. With each fevered thrust she wanted more. Wanted him deeper.

Dougal twisted his hips, rocking deeper and deeper into her softness. Her mind was mush. Colors, sounds, sensations flashed in her head. Nothing had ever felt like this before.

This was unique. This was Dougal. This felt like the missing piece of the puzzle.

Her body tingled from the top of her head to the tips of her toes. She bucked her hips up to meet his thrusts, ran her hands over his sweat-slicked skin, dug her fingernails into his muscles.

He expanded inside her, growing larger and harder until he occupied all of her. She was his. Owned, claimed, possessed.

Yes.

Every other thought left her head. There was only room for him. She wrapped her legs around his waist pulling him in deeper still. His fierce, insistent thrusts pushed her to the limits of her endurance.

They were perfectly in tune. Coupled. It was as if they'd known each other centuries instead of for just a few short days. As if she'd been waiting for this man her entire life and her life until now had been nothing but a dress rehearsal.

Unerringly he seemed to know her body. Where she ached to be stroked, how she liked to be kissed, what areas begged for pressure, which ones hungered for a soft touch.

Every stroke took her higher and higher toward her ulti

goal. It was fierce, basic, extreme, elemental. She cried his name over and over until tears rolled down her cheeks.

It was too much. Too wonderful. She didn't deserve this kind of pleasure—not when she was lying to him about who she was.

"You're crying," Dougal whispered and stopped moving. "Roxie, what's wrong? Am I hurting you?"

"No, no." She smiled at him. Emotion clogged her chest, made it hard for her to draw in air. "You're making me very happy."

"These are good tears?" He looked confused.

"The best kind," she sniffled.

He made a noise low in his throat and kissed tears from her cheeks as he began moving inside her again with soft, determined strokes.

"Ah," she murmured. "That feels so good."

He quickened his pace. They were all slippery mouths and sweaty bodies, high-speed lust.

Then he pulled his mouth from hers and flung his head back, groaning as he let out a cry of raw animal pleasure. The power of his climax took her so completely that Roxie's immediately followed.

She was tumbling, tripping, rolling into the orgasm as if it had always been her fate. She heard his groan and knew he was following her into the abyss, rocking and pumping and thrusting.

"Roxie," he called out, and the sound of her name on his lips changed her forever.

11

ALL THE WAY BACK to the Eros resort, Roxie floated on a cloud of postcoital bliss. The rays of the sun glowed brighter; the air smelled sweeter; the birds' song sounded more melodic. She had no idea sex could feel so joyful.

She sat at the back of the bus, lazily watching Dougal while Jess and Sam chatted gaily about their afternoon with their friends. She didn't hear a word they said. All she could think about was Dougal.

And then a small fissure of worry settled into the center of her chest.

This feeling was too good. Too perfect. Soon she would be leaving England, going back to her job at Getaway Airlines, never to see Dougal Lockhart again.

She found the notion far more disturbing than she should. He was nothing more than a fling. She knew that. And yet, she couldn't stop herself from wanting more. The man had gotten under her skin, and the thought of quitting him made her feel panicky. Now that she'd found him—learned what great sex was really all about—she was just supposed to give him up?

Roxie whimpered inwardly. She didn't want to, but what kind of future could she have with this man when their entire relationship was built on a lie? He didn't even know who she really was. Everything between them had been an act. A role she'd been playing. Was that what had made the sex so good?

The fact that she'd stepped outside of herself and donned a wild-woman persona?

She reached up to trace a finger over the comedy-tragedy necklace at her throat.

Who was she behind the emotional mask? Mild-mannered Roxie from Brooklyn? Or the sort of bold, brazen woman who made love in a field of wildflowers with a man she barely knew?

Although she'd only known Dougal a week, this chemistry between them ran deeper than physical desire. She'd never felt this kind of connection with anyone; it was as if he really saw her for who she was. He knew who she was at her essence and she knew him just as well. She couldn't explain it. She simply accepted that it was true.

Dougal possessed a cautious and guarded nature, but in spite of all that, she'd been able to slip past his defenses and he'd slipped past hers.

He caught her gaze as she got off the bus with the rest of the guests and her heart swooned. He winked.

Be cool. Don't show what you're feeling. You don't want to get him in trouble.

But she couldn't help herself. She winked back, sharing their little secret.

Roxie didn't know what was going to happen between them once the trip was over. Most likely nothing. But she wasn't going to let it stop her from enjoying the game right now.

Her sense of fun was shattered, however, when she returned to her room and checked the voice mail on her cell phone. Porter Langley had called. Three times. She pushed the button to review the letters in her mailbox.

"Roxie? Why do you have your cell phone turned off? Call me."

"Roxie, it's Porter again. Where are you? We need to talk."

"I really need to talk to you today. Call me back as soon as you get this message."

Sighing, she kicked off her shoes, plunked down on the big four-poster Tudor bed and punched in her boss's number.

"Where have you been?" Porter asked the minute he picked up the phone.

"Hello, Mr. Langley."

"I've been trying to call you all day."

"I've been out on an excursion."

"I'm not paying you to have a good time. Take your cell phone with you and keep it turned on."

"Now how dumb would that be?" she asked. "I wouldn't be incognito if I had to stop and answer a call from my boss every five minutes. What's so urgent?"

"Okay, okay, you're right. Listen, you know I'm in the process of courting Limerick Air."

"Yes."

"Well, they were all gung-ho last week. We were this close to inking a deal, and suddenly they're acting coy, not returning my calls, being evasive when I do talk to them. My gut tells me they've got another suitor and I'm pretty sure it's Taylor Corben," he said.

"So what do you want from me?"

"Find out for sure. If I know what's going on, it will give me more leverage."

"How am I supposed to do that?"

"Talk to the staff at Eros. Snoop around. See what you can dig up. You have my full permission to do whatever it takes. Even if that means bending a few rules or even breaking a few laws."

Roxie blew out her breath. "I'm really not comfortable with this. I'm having second thoughts about this whole thing. I hate lying and spying and—"

"It's too late for regrets," her boss snapped. "You're in this up to your neck. Find out if Taylor Corben is in negotiations with Limerick Air or you can kiss that PR position goodbye."

That's fine, tell him you quit. You're a good assistant. You can get a job anywhere. Don't let him intimidate you. You've already compromised your values. Stop before it's too late to come back.

But as much as she might want to do that, she knew she couldn't. Stacy was depending on her. She swallowed hard. "I'll do my best."

ROXIE FIGURED THE INFORMATION she needed could be found in the resort's main computer room. The investigating she'd done to date told her that the staff who worked inside the room went home at five. It would remain empty until the following morning, although getting into the room would require a little breaking and entering.

The thought of crossing the line from spy to burglar made her stomach hurt. *You're not really a burglar,* she tried to convince herself. *You're just breaking in, you're not stealing anything.*

Who was she kidding? She was stealing information. It might not be physically tangible, but it was theft all the same.

She wrestled with her conscience, torn between calling up her boss and telling him to go to hell, and the very real fact that if she lost her job, Stacy would be forced to drop out of college.

It's almost over, whispered her practical voice that had gotten her through many tough times. *Just grit your teeth and get Porter the information he wants. You'll be on your way home in a few days and then you can put this whole thing behind you.*

Of course the biggest question weighing on her mind was how to get by the locking mechanism on the door, which was like the ones used on the bungalows. They opened with an electronic key card. She'd need one to gain entry. The housekeeping staff wore their master keys on lanyards around their necks. Somehow, she was going to have to steal one.

Fresh anxiety deepened the pains shooting through her stomach and she pressed her palm against her belly. Her mind spun and she felt guilty, guilty, guilty.

If Dougal knew what she was up to… She hitched in a breath. He'd be so disappointed in her. She was disappointed in herself.

Just do it, get it over with.

Squaring her shoulders, she left her bungalow under cover of darkness and crept into the main building, her mind working out the details of how she was going to get her hands on one of the master key cards that would give her entry to the computer room.

It turned out that luck was with her. She found a housekeeping cart parked outside the computer room and the door propped open with a mop. She wouldn't have to steal a key card after all. She could slip in while the housekeeping staff was inside and find a place to hide until they left.

Still, her pulse was pounding as she eased past the mop and into the room crowded with computers and other office equipment. She heard someone cough in the room beyond the main one she'd just stepped into.

Quick, find a place to hide.

Frantically, she cast her gaze around the room and spied what appeared to be a free-standing metal supply closet with double doors. On tiptoes, she darted toward it and then twisted one of the handles. A hinge creaked. Heart pounding, she thrust herself inside with the copy paper, toner, paper clips and staples and pulled the door closed behind her. She held her breath, waiting, her heartbeat thumping loudly in her ears.

After a few seconds she slowly let out her breath, gathered up her courage and pressed one eye to the thin crack between the two doors. A minute passed, then another. Just when she thought she couldn't stand the suspense a second longer, she saw a man in a housekeeping uniform toddling around emptying the trash cans. What seemed like an eternity later, he finished up his duties, picked up his mop, clicked off the light.

Roxie stayed put for a bit longer, making sure he was truly gone. Then she eased from the closet. Her breathing had slowed, but her legs were shaking. She went to the nearest desk, clicked on a light and quickly scanned the papers stacked there. Nothing of interest. She moved to the next desk and then the next. She didn't have a system and she wasn't really certain what she was looking for or where to find it. At this rate, she'd be here all night.

Sighing, she plopped down in a chair at the last remaining desk and played the flashlight over the papers there. A green file marked Confidential caught her eye. She picked it up. The file was sealed. Did she dare open it?

Put it down, move on, directed her conscience.

But what if the very thing she needed was inside the file folder?

Knowing she really had no choice, she reached for the letter opener sticking from the container full of pens and pencils by the side of the computer monitor. With trembling fingers, she slid the letter opener underneath the sealed flap and sliced it open. She pulled the document from the file.

It took a second for her to realize what she was reading, but when she did, she understood she was facing another big dilemma.

The documents were copies of confidential financial reports about Taylor's company intended for the director of IT. These were proprietary details that would cause her boss to salivate. Should she tell him or not? That was the loaded question. She could keep her mouth shut and he would never know she found it. On the other hand, delivering this kind of information would guarantee her that promotion.

Pushing back the guilt chewing her up inside, Roxie stuffed the documents in the file folder, then stood up, lifted her blouse and shoved the folder into the waistband of her jeans. She pulled her blouse back down. Her palms were sweaty and her heart was thumping faster than ever. She needed to get out of here before she was caught.

Just as she was about to shut off the light, she noticed a calendar on the wall with something scrawled across the bottom of it. Squinting, she stepped closer to read: Taylor arrives May 22 for a stopover on her way to Dublin.

Bingo. Here was proof that Taylor was heading for Ireland. Roxie had found out far more than she'd bargained for.

DOUGAL WALKED THE CORRIDOR of the Eros resort, his nostrils filled with the sexy smell of burning incense, his ears teased by mood music, his mind wrapped tightly around Roxie. He'd come back from the trip to Cambridge in a daze, his body achy in all the right places, and he couldn't seem to stop smiling. It was almost 11 p.m., and most of the guests had retreated to their cottages for the evening.

After getting back from the day trip, he'd had a meeting with Gerry McCracken. There'd been no further incidents of sabotage, and Gerry was of the mind that the incidents weren't related, but Dougal wasn't so sure. Still, there was no evidence that tied the autopilot problems on the plane to the tampered spotlight or the beheaded water sprinklers. And by now he was completely convinced that if someone was behind the incidents, it wasn't Roxie.

That feeling of certainty stirred other feelings inside him, tender feelings that urged him to take another risk on love. With Roxie, he was finally willing to let go of the foolishness he'd felt after Ava's betrayal and take a chance on the chemistry that sizzled between him and Roxie. The trick was taking that first step and admitting to her that he wanted more.

He'd taken his dinner with the guests, and after the meal was over he made his rounds of the resort, on the lookout for anything suspicious. He found nothing out of the ordinary, and he was debating whether or not to show up at Roxie's cottage when he heard a door open, saw a swath of light fall onto the marble floor.

Not just any door, but the door leading to the nerve center of the resort—the main room that housed the computer systems, which should have been locked at this time of night. Was someone working late? Or could it be the cleaning staff?

Then a shadow crossed the doorway and the light clicked off. The hairs on Dougal's neck lifted and his gut squeezed. Something wasn't right. He stepped back into an alcove where he could watch the room without being seen. He held his breath, waited. Someone emerged.

Dougal narrowed his eyes. It was a woman—medium height, curvy, jet-black hair. She pulled the door closed behind her, looked furtively up and down the corridor and then turned for the exit.

He stepped from the alcove and called her name. "Roxie."

AT THE SOUND OF HER NAME, Roxie froze.

Footsteps hurried toward her.

Okay, don't panic. Act cool and calm. She coached herself, slipped into the role and turned to face Dougal.

"Hi!" She smiled brightly. Did she sound too cheerful? Was she trying too hard?

"Hey," he said softly, but his eyes looked troubled. "What are you doing here?"

"Um…I was just out for a walk."

"Did you need something?" He glanced toward the door of the office she'd just exited.

"Er…no…um…I was walking by and saw that the office door was open," she lied, cradling her arms across her chest so he couldn't see the outline of the file beneath the blouse.

"No one was inside," she went on, "so I just turned out the light and closed the door."

He looked as though he did not believe her.

"So," she said, anxious to distract him. "Where are you off to?"

"I was coming to see you."

"You were?"

He smiled. "I was hoping you were free for the evening."

"Um…" Her body yearned to be with Dougal again, but she was feeling far too guilty. Plus, she wanted to get this information to Mr. Langley straightaway and tell him that she'd more than delivered on her promise and now she wanted out of the spying business. "It's pretty late, maybe tomorrow night."

His eyes darkened with a meaning she could not read. "Okay."

"I had a good time today," she said.

"As did I."

If that was the case, why did he look so stiff and why did she feel so leaden? They stood looking at each other. The moment was awkward and tense. She wasn't sure what she should do or say next.

"So, good night," he finally said.

"Good night."

Was he going to kiss her? She held her breath.

But he did not. He simply touched her shoulder, gave her a wistful smile and walked away in the opposite direction.

DOUGAL LAY ON THE BED in his room in the staff quarters at the back of the castle, his mind troubled over his encounter with Roxie. Why had she been in that office? Could it be true? Had she really found the door open and just shut it to be thoughtful? He wanted to believe her.

But his certainty of her innocence had been shattered.

From the first moment he'd seen her, he'd known she was different. That she wasn't who she seemed to be. He cursed his heightened instincts that allowed him to see trouble ahead of other people. It was an important skill in the security business, but sometimes it made you see and feel and understand things you didn't want to see and feel and understand.

Roxie Stanley was up to something and he was going to do what he should have done days ago—run a thorough background check on her.

He flipped onto his other side and thought of their day punting on the Cam. It had been simply one of the best days of his life. Sadness twined through him.

When had it happened? When had he started falling for the wrong woman? When and why? He'd known better and yet he'd let it happen. No two ways about it. He was going to get hurt. Again.

Stupid, stupid.

The phone at his bedside rang. He sat up in surprise, glanced at the clock. It was two in the morning. Who was calling?

He picked it up as a bad feeling curled through him. "Hello?"

"Dougal, it's Gerry."

"What's wrong?"

"The computers have all gone down, nothing's working. We can't take reservations. It's chaos."

"At all the Eros resorts or just this one?"

"Just this one so far."

"What caused it?" he asked, trepidation creeping up his spine. "Do you think it's a virus?"

"I doubt it," Gerry said. "All the backup batteries have been shut off, as well. The whole system has crashed. It looks like we've lost everything."

FOR THE NEXT TWO DAYS, the staff worked to fix the problems caused by the crash while Dougal and Gerry talked with an expert in computer forensics to find the source of the sabotage. Their research led them to determine that someone at the resort had let a Trojan loose on the Eros system, and it had happened around the same time Dougal had discovered Roxie in the offices. But of course the Trojan horse could have been released remotely so that didn't necessarily mean someone on site had caused it.

He didn't want to believe her capable of such a thing, but the evidence was damning, although he wanted to be absolutely certain before he confronted her. Instead, he had to go on the remaining tours and pretend nothing had changed between them. He kept Taylor apprised of the developments, but stopped short of implicating Roxie, since he had no real proof it was her.

Saturday was the big finale of the scheduled events of the tour. A Renaissance Festival to end all Renaissance Festivals, and the event was open to the public. He used prepping for the event as his excuse to avoid going to Roxie's cottage every time she invited him in. Finally she stopped asking.

But he hadn't stopped wanting to go to her.

Saturday's schedule was chock-full of events from the opening parade featuring actors hired to play King Henry the Eighth and Jane Seymour. The slate included jousting, crafts, animal herding and other live dioramas depicting life in the sixteenth century—fortune-tellers, falconry, games of chance and weaponry demonstrations, including knife throwing and fencing. The minute Dougal saw Roxie dressed as a saucy serving wench, his heart flipped.

He was in big trouble. If she was the saboteur, she'd been leading him down the primrose path and he'd stupidly followed his dick where she'd led.

Roxie met his glance and quickly looked away. Dougal's pulse leaped. It was all he could do not to make his way through the crowd to her. And if Lucy Kenyon hadn't brushed past him with a worried expression on her face, he probably would have.

"Lucy," he called to her, "what's wrong?"

"It's nothing, no big deal, and you've got enough on your slate without hearing my tales of woe."

Had something else happened? He touched Lucy's arm. "Talk to me. Maybe I can help."

"The men we had coming to do the fencing clinic called in sick with food poisoning. I've been on the phone trying to find replacements, but on such short notice I'm not getting anywhere. I'm probably going to have to shut down the demonstration."

"I know how to fence," Dougal said. "I could step in."

Lucy's jaw dropped. "Seriously?"

"Seriously. So now you only need to find one replacement."

"You know what? One of the guests put down on her profile that she fences. Of course, she might not be willing to participate, but let me go ask her." Lucy hugged Dougal around the neck. "Oh, you are a lifesaver."

"When do you need me?"

"The first demonstration starts in an hour… Oh look, there she is." Lucy rushed up to Roxie.

He blinked. The guest who knew how to fence was his Roxie? *She's not your Roxie.*

"Dougal." Lucy waved him over. "Come here."

Heart thundering, he went.

"Roxie's agreed." Lucy beamed.

Roxie's gaze seared into Dougal's.

"Well," Lucy said. "I'll just leave you two alone to talk strategy and get changed into your fencing outfits. So much to do."

She fluttered off, leaving Roxie and Dougal standing together in the thick of the crowd pouring over the moat bridge onto the castle grounds.

"So," he said, "you know how to fence."

"You sound surprised."

"It's not a skill many young women possess."

"Right back at you. I've never dated a guy who fenced. I mean…um…" she stammered. "That's not what I meant. I didn't mean to imply we have any kind of relationship… I—"

"We have a relationship."

"Yes, sure, of course, but I didn't want to assume anything. This is a vacation for me, a fantasy. We might be totally different in the real world." She slapped a palm over her mouth. "I'm babbling."

He grinned. He couldn't help it. She was just so adorable. How could a woman so cute and open and vulnerable be a saboteur?

"Why don't we go get changed and pick out our equipment and do a few practice moves before the demonstration?" he suggested. "We can meet out behind the jousting area. It's isolated and we won't be interrupted."

"Yes, good, great." She still seemed a bit off balance at the prospect of fencing with him. To be honest, he was a bit nervous himself.

"It's okay," he said. "Just relax. You'll be fine."

"Thanks for calming me down. I haven't fenced in years."

"Neither have I."

"My dad was a fencer," she said as they walked toward the equipment tent. "He was all set to go to the Olympics, but my mom got pregnant with me and he decided to forgo it."

"That's impressive."

"What? That he was a potential Olympian or that he chose my mother and me over his passion for fencing?"

"Both," Dougal said.

"Dad started teaching me to fence when I was five years old. He had dreams of me following in his footsteps, but I was never that good. So, what about you? How did you get into fencing? You don't really seem the type."

"What does that mean?"

"There's something poetic about it. Romantic." She cocked

her head at him. "You don't strike me as either particularly romantic or poetic."

He splayed a hand over his heart, feigned a hurt expression. "I'm wounded, truly wounded."

"Yeah, you look utterly shattered." She laughed.

"Actually, my football coach suggested it. Said it would help my balance and coordination. It was either fencing or ballet. *That* was a no-brainer."

"Ah, football, now it all makes sense."

"I see," he teased. "So you're saying instead of romantic and poetic I'm more the cave-dwelling, Neanderthal type?"

"You said it, I didn't."

"Well, the fencing worked to refine this caveman. The year I learned to fence, our football team went to the district play-offs."

"What position did you play?"

"Wide receiver."

"Well, at least you weren't quarterback."

"What's wrong with quarterback?"

"Too much of a cliché. You're good-looking, rugged, confident. If you'd been quarterback, as well…"

"Nope, I wasn't quarterback."

"Class president?"

"Not that smart."

"Prom king?"

He hung his head. "Guilty as charged."

"I knew it," she crowed.

"From the way you're scoffing, I take it you weren't head cheerleader, class president or prom queen," he said.

"Not even close."

"You hung out in the library."

"And proud of it." She lifted her chin.

"Really? Because from where I'm standing, you should have owned that high school."

"A lot of things can change in ten years. In high school I had braces and I was horribly shy. The two places I felt like my true self was when I was on stage pretending to be someone else or when I had an épée in my hand."

He narrowed his eyes and leaned in so close he could smell the scent of her soap. "You're quite the mystery, Roxanne Stanley."

"No more so than you, Dougal Lockhart."

"Touché."

"Pun intended?"

"An insider fencing pun," he confirmed.

They weaved through the crowd. At just after nine in the morning, the place was already packed; excitement rippled through the air. On the way to the equipment tent, they passed the fencing area. A banner overhead proclaimed, Classical Fencing: The Martial Art of Incurable Romantics.

That made Dougal smile. He'd told Roxie he'd taken fencing at his football coach's suggestion and that was true, but he'd had a secondary reason for taking up the sport. The martial art component appealed to him. Not that he was an incurable romantic by any means. Rather he'd been interested in the weaponry. Fencing was just another fighting technique in his arsenal. During high school, before he'd switched to football, he'd taken up boxing and been a Golden Gloves contender. He'd become proficient at Krav Maga, and he'd been a wickedly good marksman long before he'd entered the military.

The thing was, Dougal had been dedicated to taking care of his mother, especially after her loser boyfriend had cleaned out their bank account and skipped town. He flashed back to the memory of the ten-year-old kid he'd been, helplessly patting his mother on the shoulder, trying to comfort her as she sobbed her heart out.

It had been a pivotal moment. He'd already been trying to fill his father's shoes after the old man had abandoned them two years earlier, but seeing his normally strong, practical mother dissolve into tears made Dougal realize what a poor job he'd been doing. Mowing the lawn, taking out the trash, helping her cook dinner wasn't enough. He had to step up to the plate and learn how to protect her.

The next day he'd asked her to enroll him in boxing classes and she'd agreed. And he'd spent the rest of his life trying to be a good and honorable man.

"I'm worried," Roxie whispered, leaning against his shoulder.

He shifted toward her. "What about?"

"It's been so long since I've fenced, and I'm not exactly in peak physical condition."

Dougal drew a languid gaze over her body. "I wouldn't say that," he drawled.

She swatted his arm. "You know what I mean. You're Mr. Bulked Up, and the most exercise I get is walking from the subway to the office. Granted it's ten blocks, and I often take the stairs to the sixth floor, but still…it probably won't take much to wind me."

"You did fine at ballroom dancing the other night."

She pondered that. "I guess I did."

"You're probably in better shape than you think you are."

They stepped into the equipment tent, and Dougal explained to the property clerk they were taking over the fencing demonstration. The guy led them over to the weaponry section.

"Which shall we spar with?" she asked, running her hands over the hilt of the weapons lined up in a wooden rack. "Foil, épée or saber?"

"I never learned to use the foil."

She stared at him as if he'd said something blasphemous. "You've got to be kidding. Everyone starts with the foil."

"Not at my high school. Our coaches decided right off the bat which weapon suited you because they needed to train fencers quickly for interscholastic competition. Besides, the foil just didn't suit me. I'm too large."

"Ah, I get it. You're one of those guys who believe the foil is for girls."

"I don't." He did, but he wasn't going to tell her that when she was standing there with a saber in her hand.

"You were misinformed," she said.

"There are too many rules with the foil. It's unrealistic. You couldn't use foil rules in a real fight. You'd be killed."

She made a *tsk, tsk* noise with her tongue. "You miss the point entirely."

"Pun intended?"

"It's going to be one of those days, isn't it? Don't try to charm your way out of a lecture. You know you're wrong."

He chuckled, beguiled by her inflexibility on the topic. "I'm wrong, huh?"

"Here's the secret of the foil," she said. "Pay attention because this is the key to fencing with all weaponry. The foil teaches you *personal control.* Control yourself and you control your opponent. The rules teach you how to think logically in combat. Having been in the military you should understand that. The rules are based on truth. You attack when you have a clear opportunity and you defend when threatened."

"Your girl is right." The clerk nodded. "Dead-on."

"That's a matter of opinion," Dougal countered. What he wanted to say, but didn't was, "Who asked you, buddy?" See? That showed personal control.

The clerk shrugged. "I'm guessing you two will be going with the saber?"

"Obviously." Roxie rolled her eyes. "Since it's the only thing he knows how to handle."

"Hey, if you can handle a saber, you don't need anything else."

Why was he feeling so defensive? Was it because in his heart he knew she was right? That he hadn't learned personal control?

"Everything is not about brute force, as I'll soon school you," she said.

They collected their gear—fencing jacket, a mask, a glove, the underarm and chest protectors and shoes—and went into the changing room. They emerged a few minutes later. Then, with sabers in hand, went to the quiet spot behind the wooden bleachers set up for the big joust scheduled for later that day.

Grinning at each other, they squared off on the soft ground.

"En garde," Roxie said, using the fencing equivalent of "On your mark."

They lowered their masks and struck their positions, sword outstretched, one leg forward.

"Prêt," she said, meaning "Get set."

Dougal's muscles tensed.

"Allez." Roxie lunged, taking him off guard with her ferocity. It was saber play, so naturally attacks were fast and furious, but after her speech about personal control, he did not expect such immediate flurry.

Dougal parried in defense, moving his weapon to push aside her attacking blade. He immediately followed with a riposte, and it was Roxie's turn to parry.

The sound of their clashing blades rent the air, clacking and clanging.

She stamped her front foot on the ground, producing a sound known as an appel. The intention was to startle him. He anticipated the lunge, raised his saber to meet hers, gliding it down her blade, keeping her in constant contact.

They went at it in a free-for-all. The sound of their meeting weapons filled the air.

She looked so mysterious, dressed in the white outfit, the mask hiding her features and he loved the way the material of her fencing pants clung to her curvaceous thighs. A sexual thrill jolted through him, but he had no time to enjoy it. Relentlessly she came at him.

Dougal defended.

Roxie lunged.

He parried. Enough of this. He was taking control. Dougal countered, lunging hard, sending her back.

Or so he thought.

But it was a feint tactic and he hadn't seen it coming. She caught him unaware with the feint-deceive, doubling back to hit him with the completion of her lunge.

"Touché." She'd earned a point.

He'd gone for the full-on aggressive speed and power. She'd finessed him by moving around on the tactical wheel, not following the conventional moves. The woman was amazing.

"Foil fencing is for girls, huh?" Roxie came at him with a fluidity that stole his breath.

And just like that he was back on the defensive.

"I think you're lying," he said, in a flurry of blade activity. His goal was to knock her off guard with a provocative statement. Everyone was lying about something.

His ploy worked. She fumbled, letting down her guard for a split second and the edge of his saber clipped her shoulder, giving him the right-of-way and a point.

"One-one," he said.

Her breasts rose as she chuffed out a breath of air, just before she attacked again. He felt the tension in her blade; something had changed. She'd lost focus.

"Give up the deception, Roxie. Admit the truth." He scored another hit and she let out a cry of frustration. "I know your secret."

"Huh?" She hesitated.

He scored another point. "Touché."

"Dammit," she mumbled.

"About that secret…" Their sabers clashed.

"I don't have any secrets." Her voice sounded reedy, breathless.

"I know you're lying," he said, attempting to rattle her into telling him the truth right here, right now.

"Okay," she chuffed. "You've got me."

He held his breath. *Was she going to confess?*

"I *have* fenced since high school."

"I knew it," Dougal went on, in spite of the disappointment knotting his chest.

She recovered from her slipups, returning full force, dazzling him with fancy footwork, her mental strategy, her lightness of action, her point control.

And just like that, she scored again.

They dueled in a smooth, loose rhythm as if they'd been fencing together for decades. Thrust and parry. Lunge and defend. Feint and deceive. It was like great sex with all their clothes on.

By the end of their allotted time, they were flagging and breathing heavily. Roxie seemed to be losing steam—her saber wasn't held as high as previously. He had her if he wanted to take her.

Did he want to do her in? His killer instincts said yes.

Unless this was another deception.

They rounded on each other. She was weakening. His competitive instincts, his familiarity with the saber, his desire to prove her wrong about the foil drove him in for the final point of the match.

He lunged with the brute force, take-your-opponent-down-as-soon-as-possible strategy he'd been taught.

Roxie parried, sank back.

Dougal came on strong, prepared for her riposte. It didn't come. Aha, he had her for sure. He made one final lunge.

And suddenly the tip of her saber was centered squarely at his breastplate.

He stared down in disbelief, the pressure of her weapon pressing against his chest. How had that happened?

"The true art of fencing," Roxie gloated, triumphantly ripping off her mask, her face flushed, her black hair spilling over her shoulders, her blue eyes snapping with delight, "is to make the other guy run into your point."

12

"GREAT JOB," DOUGAL TOLD HER after their last demonstration of the day as they were returning their supplies to the equipment tent. "You put me through my paces."

"Thank you." She smiled. "I really enjoyed it."

He looked at her and he just knew she simply could not be involved in the stuff he feared she was involved in. His gut and his heart were urging him onward, even if his mind was telling him to be cautious. No matter why she'd been in that office, he was sure she had a good reason. A reason unrelated to the computer sabotage. He couldn't deny his need for her. It overrode everything else. He had to have her. Had to speak with her. They needed a long, intimate talk to clear the air.

"You know," he said, "this is our last real evening together. The flight leaves at 6 a.m. on Monday."

"I know."

"I was hoping we'd get to spend it together." Damn if he didn't feel as nervous as a schoolboy. She looked into his eyes, and Dougal's gut sent him that same message it had that first day on the plane: *She's the one you've been waiting for.*

"I'd like that. We can order room service."

He reached out to touch her arm. "I was wondering…" He trailed off, not knowing how to broach the subject.

"Yes?"

"If it could just be you and me."

"Of course."

"No," he said. "Just you and me making love. No props, no costumes, no role-playing. Just Roxie and Dougal unplugged. Honest, open. No secrets. No hidden agendas."

She looked decidedly nervous, although he was determined not to read anything into it. "But...but I thought you liked our role-playing."

"I do," he said. It was just that they'd been donning so many masks he wasn't sure who the real Roxie was, and before he made up his mind to extend this relationship outside the realm of Eros, he wanted her to be herself with him. No roles, no guises, nothing to hide behind. "But for tonight I'd like it to just be us."

"Um...okay."

"Sevenish?"

"That sounds great."

ROXIE COULDN'T BELIEVE how nervous she felt. The thought of making love with Dougal without the armor of costumes scared the dickens out of her. She'd be fully opening herself up to him. What if plain old Roxie couldn't please him the way Muse or Lady Sarah or Dungeon Dominatrix or Elizabeth Bennet or apple-eating Eve could?

To help calm her nerves, she took a hot bath with lavender soap and sipped a cup of chamomile tea.

She'd just dried off and gotten dressed then when the doorbell rang. She ran a hand through her hair to smooth it and scurried to wrench open the door. It was Dougal with the room-service cart.

"Hey." Dougal wriggled two fingers at her.

"Hi," she smiled.

"You smell good."

"So do you."

He set up their meal in front of the window with a view of

the gardens. She giggled when he took the lid off the platters, revealing chicken Marsala, tossed salad, bruschetta and walnut brownies for dessert. To wash it all down, they shared a bottle of rosé. They sat nibbling off each other's plates like longtime lovers.

"I hate that our time together is coming to an end," he said.

"So do I." She dabbed her mouth with her napkin. "But I had no expectations beyond this."

"Really?" He looked as if he didn't believe her.

"I had a great time with you, and I think you had a great time with me. We can just leave it at that. You don't have to make me any promises."

"What if I don't want to leave it at that?"

She inhaled sharply. *Don't toy with me,* she wanted to say, but instead she just said, "Oh?"

He reached across the table and took her hands in his. "I…it's been a long time since I've had such fun with anyone."

His gaze sizzled straight through her, melting any resolve she had about keeping things casual. When had she started hungering for more? This wasn't good. The sexy environment of Eros's resort had put romantic notions into her head. Notions that had no place in her real life. When Dougal found out the truth about her… Roxie gulped. How had she ended up in this fix?

Suddenly he let go of her, pushed his hand through his hair. "You…you don't feel the same way. Aw, hell, I'm an idiot."

"No, no, I had a wonderful time. It's just that you're an Eros employee. I'm on vacation. It's—"

"A bad idea. You're right." He looked as if she'd drop-kicked him.

She felt as though she'd drop-kicked herself. If she wasn't here under such sneaky pretenses then she might have had the romance of her life. As it was, fantastic sex was the very best she could hope for. But when she looked at him she couldn't stop herself from longing for more, wishing she could have a real relationship with him. God, she'd messed things up so badly.

"This is hard for me," he said.

"And you think it's a cakewalk for me?"

"No, I don't, but I think we owe it to ourselves to fully explore the potential here."

"Dougal, I…"

But she got no further. Dougal pulled her to her feet and clamped his mouth over hers, and she was lost. Roxie's body awakened like Sleeping Beauty's to Prince Charming's kiss. No wait, scratch that. She'd promised no role-playing. She was Roxie awakening to Dougal's kiss.

Suddenly she was aware of everything, all her senses attuned. Dougal tightened the embrace, crushing her soft breasts against his muscled chest. There was no missing the hardness of his erection.

This was wrong. This was crazy. There was no cause to compound the problem. Why was she kneading her fingers along his spine? Why was she throwing back her head, exposing her throat to his hungry mouth? This could only end badly. She tried to wriggle away, but it was a tepid effort. She'd waited years for someone like him to come along, and she didn't want to fight it.

His teeth nipped lightly at the tender skin underneath her chin. Like an arrow to a bull's-eye, he'd found her secret erogenous zone. She sucked in a breath. How could this be wrong when he seemed to know exactly what to do to turn her inside out?

Just when he had her writhing mindlessly in his arms, Dougal pulled back and stared down into her face, his eyes black with a lusty sheen. "You're so beautiful."

She felt her cheeks heat. She'd always thought her skin was too pale, her nose too small, her cheeks too round to be classically beautiful, but the way he looked at her made her feel like the most attractive woman on earth.

In that moment she forgot about why this was wrong. All she could think about was how much she wanted him. Roxie ached to feel his hands skimming over her bare skin, longed to hear him call out her name in the throes of ecstasy.

He was everything she'd ever dreamed of. She could live the adventures she'd had to put on hold to raise Stacy. Her secret desires, right here, right now—it was all within her grasp. But no matter how she might wish otherwise, this relationship couldn't end well.

"I want you so badly I can't breathe," Dougal whispered. "I want to make love to you tonight, slow, soft and easy. I can't stop thinking about you, Roxie."

"Dougal…" She should say no, but when it came to him she was so weak.

"Please," he cajoled, and then he kissed her again and she knew the time for total honesty had passed. Her body swirled with need. Stunned, she realized she didn't care about the consequences. All she wanted was to have him here, now, and not think about tomorrow.

Still kissing her, Dougal guided her down the hallway and waltzed her to the bed. He eased her onto the duvet, his mouth never leaving hers. His fingers undid the buttons of her blouse. He slipped it off her shoulders, then skimmed his palms over her back to coax open the clasp of her bra.

While he was undressing her, she was frantically clawing at his shirt.

"Hey, hey," he said, finally tugging his lips from hers. "Slow down. Soft and easy, remember." The gentle expression in his eyes lit her up inside. "I want to savor this."

She pulled her bottom lip up between her teeth and whimpered.

He chuckled. "Never fear, sweetheart. We'll get there. Just give me time to pull out all my best moves."

She reached for the snap of his jeans just when his mouth

found hers again and branded her with fresh, sizzling kisses. He shucked off his pants and boxer briefs, and it wasn't until then that she realized somewhere along the way he'd kicked off his shoes. He stood on the floor; she sat on the edge of the bed, her heels hooked over the bed rail.

"What happened," she whispered, tracing the puckered scar at the top of his right thigh. She'd seen it before, but had never asked him about it because it seemed too personal a question, but if they were on the verge of taking things to the next level, she wanted to know.

"Huh?" He blinked groggily and saw where she was staring.

She reached out a hand to touch the silvered wound, but he flinched, stepped back. "Don't."

"You were shot?" She looked up to meet his eyes.

"Yes."

She wanted to ask him what had happened, but the look on his face warned her off. She dropped her gaze and instead took in the sight of his jutting, erect penis. It was a glory to behold.

Here in the soft glow from the bedroom light, she could appreciate just how gorgeous he was. Lowering her head, she lightly touched her tongue to his tip.

Dougal hissed out a long breath as if he'd been scalded. "Oh, yeah, that feels so sweet."

She took him in her mouth.

"As good as that feels, sweetheart, if you keep that up I won't last a minute."

Roxie drew back, looked up at him, at his scarred leg, his flat abdomen, his naked chest, his broad shoulders and then up to his dark eyes. He was so masculine. So strong.

Lower and lower she kissed, headed for dangerous territory.

He threaded his fingers through her hair. "No, no," he protested weakly.

"Yes…" She kissed him. "Yes."

Another kiss.

Then her hand was on him, stroking his throbbing head.

Roxie dipped her head and she tasted his flesh. Instantly wet heat gushed through her body. The muscles deep within her pelvis tightened. Her heart beat faster, and she surprised herself by how quickly she grew slick.

She slid down the length of his body, savoring the salty taste of his hot skin—tasting, licking, exploring the mysteries of his body.

He moaned when her lips closed over his shaft. He tasted so good! She felt an electrical current run through her as she licked him and reveled in her feminine power.

She loved him with her mouth, caressed him with her tongue, coaxing him to the edge of ecstasy. His body was as tense as stone.

"Not yet," he whispered. "Not yet. I want to be inside you."

"Come here," she said.

He didn't protest when she took his hand and pulled him down on the bed beside her. His eyes were dark with lust, and she spied goose bumps tracking up his arm. She grinned wickedly.

Now where had she put that condom? A quick search and she discovered it had slid onto the other side of the duvet while she'd been undressing him. She tore open the packet with her teeth, and palmed the round rubber ring.

She stood up only to discover her legs quivered like running water. She quickly turned and straddled his knees, her own knees digging into the covers.

He'd braced himself on his elbows and was watching her intently. He was the most beautiful specimen of manhood she'd ever seen, and she could hardly believe he was here with her.

His eyes met hers and his gaze was so raw, so primal, she had to look away and calm herself before she could proceed.

Trying to look casual, as if she did this all the time, Roxie ran her hand up his thigh.

He groaned and the sound served to resurrect her hunger.

Tentatively she reached out and stroked one finger down his chest, while the other hand—the one with the palmed condom—went up to touch the head of his cock.

He felt heavy and large in her hand. She thrilled to his bigness. Dougal's penis was at once velvet soft and hard as steel, an erotic combination of texture and heat. She could feel the blood pulsating through his shaft.

He groaned again, and she felt more than saw him fall back against the pillows. She took her time. Touching, kneading, stroking. He moved his hips. She could feel the muscles of his buttocks tighten. He wanted to thrust.

Teasing, she lowered her mouth to his tip.

"Don't…" he warned. "I want to be inside you and if you put your mouth around me, I'll blow it."

"Just a little taste," she said and swirled her tongue around the head of his penis.

He sucked air into his lungs in an audible gasp. She could feel him struggling to hold on to his restraint. "Roxie…"

The taste of him was both savory and sweet. A unique flavor, all Dougal. She licked him like an ice-cream cone, seeking to arouse but not to set off an inferno.

She stroked his balls while she licked, and his body stiffened. "Do you like that?"

His answer was nothing more than a hard grunt and a short, rough nod. She played with him a bit longer, feeling his penis grow to an impossible length.

When his balls pulled up tightly against his shaft she knew it was time to pull back, let his heart rate settle down.

"Roxie…" He breathed her name, pure awe in his voice. "You're a vicious goddess."

She rocked back on her heels, grinned at him.

"Come here." He pulled her into his arms.

"Wait." She moved back just enough to roll the condom down over his erection.

"Now," he said. It was a command, not a request. "Get on top of me."

Her knees were anchored on either side of his waist and she was dripping wet for him. He wrapped his hand around her neck, tugged her head down to plant a hot kiss on her mouth.

Roxie melted into him. He tasted like her, and she tasted like him. It was a sexy combination that fired her up all over again.

He settled his hands on her hips and guided her down on top of him. They both hissed out air in unison as he filled her up and she engulfed him.

She set the pace, slow and deliberate, driving him mad.

"Hurry," he urged.

"Nope," she murmured. "Payback's a bitch."

"You've got a cruel side, babe."

"It'll be worth the wait," she promised.

"Two can play this game," he said, and roguishly reached up to pinch her nipples between this thumbs and index fingers.

Fire shot down her nerve endings from her breasts to her feminine core. "Devil," she dared.

"Don't forget it." He laughed.

He moved beneath her, arching his hips, thrusting her high. His hands roved over her waist, her back, her belly and back to her breasts. At some point it felt as if he had a dozen maddening hands.

She tried to hold him off, to make him wait as long as possible, but then the clever man slipped his fingers between her legs and found her pleasure spot.

"No fair," she cried weakly, but all she got in response was a wicked chuckle.

He wriggled his finger and she couldn't hold off any longer. She rode him as if her life depended on it.

Then just before she was about to have her mind-blowing orgasm, he placed both palms around the sides of her head and pulled her down to stare deeply into her eyes.

They gazed straight into each other's souls.

At the same moment, he thrust as hard into her as he could, and the earth shifted and Roxie spiraled out of control.

His face contorted, but he never stopped looking at her, never stopped thrusting her over the edge until they both exploded in simultaneous bliss.

Her body spasmed. Jerked.

He clutched her to him. He was shaking all over.

Roxie collapsed against his chest, heard the thunderous pounding of his heart.

He squeezed her tight, kissed her all over, her eyelids, her nose, her cheeks, her chin. Then finally he found her mouth and kissed her with a joy that forever captured her heart.

SOMETIME LATER, SHE AWAKENED clutched tight in the circle of Dougal's arms.

"You awake?" he asked.

"Uh-huh."

"I've been lying here listening to you sleep. I love the way you breathe when you're sleeping. It's a soft little purring kind of noise."

"Are you saying I snore?" she teased.

"Not at all. It's just the nicest sound. Like you're completely relaxed, totally trusting."

"Hmm," she murmured.

He reached over and threaded his fingers through hers. "There's something I want to tell you."

"Does it have anything to do with the bullet wound on your thigh?" she asked.

"Yes," he said. "It does."

"Oh."

"I haven't been with a woman since—" he swallowed audibly "—since I got shot."

"How long ago?"

"Eighteen months."

"It's been a long time for me, as well," she said. "Much longer than eighteen months."

"The last time I felt this way...the way I'm feeling about you. Well...let's just say my feelings were unreliable."

"You're scared the same thing is happening with me that happened to you with this other woman?"

He hesitated, shifted. She could tell this wasn't easy for him. He wasn't the kind of guy who readily talked about his feelings.

"I'm listening," she coaxed.

A long moment ensued, and finally he ventured, "Before I went to work for Eros, I was a captain in the Air Force, specializing in aviation security."

"Uh-huh." She nodded encouragingly.

"I was stationed in Germany, and I was in charge of guarding the Air Force fleet."

"Sounds like a lot of responsibility."

"It was." He paused again, wiped a hand across his mouth before continuing. She squeezed the hand that still held hers. He gave her a wan smile. "I met a woman there. Her name was Ava, and I fell for her like an avalanche."

Jealousy, hot and unexpected, poured over her.

"By nature I'm not a particularly trusting guy. I tend to see the darker side of people, but with Ava, I was blind. I ignored my gut, which told me she wasn't all she seemed."

Roxie could tell that this was headed in a bad direction. She made a noise of sympathy at the back of her throat.

You should tell him. Tell him right now. About Langley, about Stacy, about spying for Getaway Airlines. Roxie opened her mouth, but she couldn't force out the words that she knew would ruin everything.

"We slept together, and I thought I was in love." Dougal shook his head. "One day I caught her going through my office. She pretended that she'd come there to set up a romantic scenario, but that was when the first suspicions started to creep in. I didn't want to believe she was up to something. I ignored my instincts."

"She was using you."

Dougal nodded. "I had her investigated and I discovered she was working for a terrorist cell. She'd stolen classified information from my locked files. I still don't know how she managed to get access to them, but I managed to stop her cohorts as they were rigging up a bomb in one of the planes that was due to carry military brass back to the Pentagon. Ava showed up while I was in the middle of arresting them, and she shot me in the thigh."

Roxie splayed a palm over her mouth.

"I felt like such a fool." Dougal's voice turned hard. "When my tour of duty was over, I left the Air Force. I couldn't do my job effectively. Not when I could allow my heart to rule my head. I'm telling you this because it's been very hard for me to trust a woman ever since then. But I trust you, Roxie, and that's a huge thing for me to admit."

You have to tell him the truth. You have to tell him now!

His sincere dark eyes sliced right through her. If she told him, though, she'd lose her job and then Stacy would drop out of school.

"But you, Roxie." His whisper was husky. "*You* make me want to try again."

His honesty, the vulnerability all over his face clawed at her. She was a horrible person for deceiving him, and he didn't deserve to be treated this way. "Dougal, there's some—"

But before she could work up the courage to tell him her dark secret, his lips were on hers. He slipped his arms around her, lifted her up, kissed her tenderly as if she was the most precious thing on earth.

Lust swamped her. She had to have him again. Had to have him or she would surely die. She ran her tongue around his lips, and he made a masculine noise of enjoyment.

She moaned, loving yet hating the sweet torture. She wriggled into him, her breasts pressed flush against his muscled chest.

Tell him.

He ran his fingers up and down her shoulders. She threw back her head, and he trailed his kisses to the underside of her neck, nuzzling and nibbling.

Experimentally he rubbed his thumbs over her nipples and they beaded so tight that they ached.

"Ah," he said. "So you like that?"

"It feels awesome."

A hazy hotness draped over her, thick with sexual urgency. She wanted him so badly that her need was a solid, unyielding mass in her throat.

"What about this?" His tongue laved the underside of her jaw.

She shuddered against him.

"And this?" Lightly he tickled the skin on the inside of her upper arm.

"Wild man." She gasped.

"Exactly." He grinned.

When his mouth found its way back to hers again, Roxie could hear nothing except for the tyranny of her beating heart. The force of his desire caused her to tremble and sweat. Her knees quivered. Her heart pounded.

He tunneled his fingers through her hair. She felt his presence in every cell of her body, in every breath she took, in every strum of the blood pumping through her veins.

This new sensation drove her into a frenzy. Her muscles flexed. Blinding flashes of light. The rushing sound of ocean waves in her head. Uncontrollable spasms rattled her body.

Her world quaked.

Madly, frantically, they grappled with each other. His hands were broad and warm. His mouth an instrument of exquisite torture. Time spun, morphed, as elusive as space.

The entire time he was buried inside of her, he stared deeply into her eyes, as if he was lost in her gaze and could not find his way out. Did not even want to find his way out.

They were one. Mated. Trembling and clinging to each other.

His cock filled her up, pushing deep inside of her until he could go no farther.

Then he pulled back. In and out, he moved in a smooth rhythm that rocked her soul. He rode her and she rode him until they both came in a searing white blinding light.

And all she could think of was that she could never have him for her own.

13

DOUGAL HEARD ROXIE padding quietly against the tile floor before he saw her.

He stood at the stove whipping up a big breakfast. Eros had fully stocked the kitchenette with everything a romantic chef would need. When he was growing up, his mother had insisted he learn how to cook, so Dougal could flip a mean Denver omelet.

After last night, he and Roxie needed sustenance. They must have burned a thousand calories. He was going to feed her and then he was going to make love to her all over again. He'd made her come four times the night before—a personal best for him—and he was eager to shoot for number five.

Cooking for her spurred his urge to nourish Roxie in every way possible.

Hearing her approach above the noisy sizzle of the bacon and hissing steam from the espresso machine, he knew she was going to wrap her arms around his waist before he even felt her petite palms slide across his belly.

Dougal set the spatula on the granite countertop and turned into her embrace, pulling her close to him for a kiss. She tasted pepperminty and wore silky pink pajamas without a bra.

"Good morning," he murmured against her lips.

He could feel her nipples bead up against his chest. He cupped Roxie's butt. No panty lines. She was totally naked underneath that silk.

Instantly his cock hardened.

Don't burn the bacon. They'd been in bed for over twelve hours. They needed to eat so they could hit the sack for another twelve. While he thanked heavens it was Sunday, that meant tomorrow was Monday and they'd be flying home. It was over.

"Well." She chuckled and pressed herself tighter against his erection. "Good morning to you, too."

"I can't help it," he said. "See what you do to me?"

She blushed prettily, which was amazing since they'd just done some very intimate things together. She really was quite bashful.

"Breakfast is ready. I hope you're hungry."

"Starved," she said. "Although it looks like you made enough food to feed the entire tour group."

"No way, babe. Today it's just you and me. Have a seat."

She pulled out a chair at the quaint little bistro table in front of the picture window. "Whatever it is you're cooking, it smells heavenly."

"Not as heavenly as you."

She lowered her lashes and sent him a coy half smile— sassy but demure, Snow White through and through. Something hitched his chest. An emotion he couldn't identify. The feeling was at once hot and sweet and uncomfortable.

He realized he wanted much more than sex from Roxie, and at the same time, he knew that circumstances were such that he could never have it. The sudden loneliness that stabbed through him was as sharp as it was unexpected.

Dougal set their plates, loaded up with omelets, bacon and biscuits on the table. Roxie angled her head and her dark hair swung fetchingly over her shoulders like a shimmery black curtain. Grinning, she rubbed her palms together. "It's been ages since anyone has cooked for me. I feel pampered. Thank you."

"No problem. I like to cook."

"You are an enigma, Dougal Lockhart. A guy's guy who knows his way around a kitchen. Tell me again why you're not married?"

"Never found the right girl." He produced two forks from the silverware drawer, napkins from the pantry and butter from the fridge. Steam rose from the coffee cups he parked beside the plates. He plunked down across from her, happy to notice she was digging into the omelet with gusto.

"Mmm." She made a sexy noise of pure pleasure. "Seriously, if you ever decide to give up the tour-guide business, you could have an amazing career in food service."

"Good to know I have options," he said, feeling pleased that he'd pleased her.

"I get the impression that you're skilled at a lot of things." She cut a pat of butter from the stick and slipped it between the folds of her biscuit. "Are these homemade?"

He nodded. "My mother's recipe."

She sat looking at him with her intense blue eyes, and he just came unraveled. He reached for her at the same moment she dropped her fork to her plate with a clatter and leaned across the table toward him.

"Dougal." She breathed in.

He exhaled. "Roxie."

His brain fogged. The smell of her tangled in his nose and drove him wild. He acted purely on instinct. His dick was as hard as the granite countertop. In fact, he was going to take her on that countertop. Spread her legs and do her right there.

The next thing he knew they were naked and he was sheathed in a condom, bending her over the counter, and entering her from behind. She was slick and ready for him.

"You're so wet." He groaned and sank in deeper.

Trembling, he wrapped his arms around her waist, dropped his forehead to her shoulder blade and closed his eyes to savor her tightness. Dougal could hardly think. His mind was obliterated by the feel of her around him. His emotions blistered hot, intense and unexpected.

Frantically he pumped into her. There was no smooth landing, no easy glide. Dougal was on a jet plane headed straight to the ground, spinning out into the clear blue sky. His whole body shook, and sweat slicked his back. He was helplessly out of control. It scared him while at the same time he felt utterly blissful. What in the hell was happening to him? He'd never ever been this rough, this rushed.

Then from out of nowhere, he felt her fingertips caress his balls and boom!

One tickle and he came. Just a simple light scratch from her soft hand and he detonated. He stiffened against her, his hips arching, grinding so hard against her, the fluid poured out of him, his cock so hot and drained he thought he'd disintegrate.

Blindly he clung to Roxie, squeezing her tightly as if she was the only thing keeping him from falling apart.

He cursed himself. "I'm sorry, I'm sorry," he apologized. "I've never gone off like that."

"Shh," she whispered, separating them, turning in his arms to cradle his head between her hands and kiss his lips. "It's okay."

"It's not. I'm a rude, selfish bastard and I—"

"I like it that I can make you lose control." She ran her fingers over his face. "It makes me feel feminine and powerful."

Maybe that's what scared him so much. He'd always been in control with women. He'd never lost it like this. Why was it happening? What did it mean?

He was still rock hard. He cupped her buttocks and lifted her up on the counter, entered her from the front and rocked against her. Dishes clattered to the floor. Silverware flew under the table. They didn't notice. She moaned and tossed back her head. She sank her fingers into his hair, directed his head to her breasts.

"Suck my nipples," she commanded.

He did as Roxie asked, taking first one pink, straining nipple into his mouth, then the other, lightly nibbling each one until she moaned again.

He wouldn't have thought it possible, but he grew even harder inside of her.

Her muscles tightened around him. Groaning, he fisted a hand through her hair and pulled her head back, plied his teeth and lips and tongue along the silky column of her long, slender throat.

Dougal's nerve endings tingled. His heart thumped. His lungs chuffed. His belly burned with damaging need. Forget control. Trying to gather it was a lost cause. *He* was a lost cause. He was going to blow again and he still hadn't made her come.

No way was he going to let that happen.

With a supreme effort of will, he eased back and slipped his hand down to where she was stretched tight around him. His fingers tangled in the soft damp hairs at her feminine entrance. He found her clitoris, and she hissed in her breath as he lightly brushed the pad of his index finger over the swollen nub.

He captured her mouth with his at the same time as he increased the pressure, swallowed up her startled gasp. A hot wire of excitement flashed down his spine straight to his groin. He pushed inside her warm box again, all the while still stroking her twitching hood.

Pinning her to the counter with his body, his tongue deep in her mouth, he thrust into her hard and fast.

And felt the rising rumble overtake him at the same time as she let out a thin, strangled sound.

Lost. They were lost together in this beautiful, splendid world.

Grinding and aching, clutching and shaking, they shot into orbit together.

Something inside Dougal broke loose, cracked open, shattered. He was raw, primal, exposed.

Ah, hell, he thought.

All the energy left his body in one exhausted release, leaving him spent.

Roxie was nothing—*nothing*—like any other woman he'd ever experienced. She was something else entirely.

Dougal's eyes misted and his nose burned. He clenched his jaw tight, blinking back the onslaught of emotions. He pressed his face into her hair, heaved in a shuddering breath, closed his eyes and held her close while his heart rate slowed.

"Thank you," Roxie gasped. "That was exactly what I needed. Straight-up wild sex with absolutely no strings attached."

No strings.

She was letting him off the hook, setting him free. That should be great news. He should be happy.

But he wasn't.

"You're the best I've ever had," she whispered, pressing her mouth against his ear. "Not that I've had a lot of experience, but you're definitely an A plus."

Something every man longed to hear, but it sounded so hollow. All he could think was *no strings attached.*

He wanted to find the sturdiest ball of twine he could get his hands on and bind her to him forever.

That's when Dougal knew he was in serious trouble.

WHY HAD SHE SAID WHAT she'd said about no strings attached? She wanted strings and lots of them. She wanted a whole yarn barn full of strings.

But she couldn't have them. She'd made love to him under false pretenses, hiding the reason she was really on this tour. Spying and betraying Dougal's confidence to Porter Langley, a man she was rapidly losing respect for.

Dougal looked at her with eyes so sad she feared he could read her thoughts. Misery moved into her heart, set up house.

She dropped her gaze, grabbed up her pajamas and scrambled into them. She was a horrible person, and she should just come clean right now and take her punishment.

Dougal pulled on his pants, zipped them up. "Roxie?"

"Yes?" She plunked down in the chair to slip on her socks.

Dougal took the chair next to her, rested his palm on her forearm. "Look at me."

Reluctantly she lifted her head.

"I've got something I need to tell you." His tone was serious. "I haven't been completely honest with you."

A lump the size of Alaska chunked up in her throat. "You've got a girlfriend," she quipped. *Please don't let him have a girlfriend.*

"I don't have a girlfriend."

"Whew, that's good. I didn't want some chick chasing me down to yank my hair out for fooling around with her man."

"I would never do that. When I'm with a woman, I'm with her." His hand was still on her forearm.

"Oh," she said, not knowing what else to say. *Be with me.* That's what she wanted to say, but of course, she couldn't.

"I'm going to have to ask you to keep what I'm about to tell you in strictest confidence. Can you promise me that, Roxie?" His intense gaze pinned her to the spot.

She couldn't promise him that, not when her job and Stacy's future might depend on sharing the information with her boss. "Dougal, I…"

"I can trust you." He interlaced his fingers with hers, squeezed her hand.

Compelled by the vulnerable expression on his face, Roxie nodded mutely. She couldn't help feeling flattered that he trusted her, especially after what had happened to him with that other woman.

"I'm not really a tour guide."

She laughed nervously. "What do you mean?"

He leaned forward, shoulders tense, his eyes never leaving hers. "I'm a private duty air marshal undercover as a tour guide. I own my own security firm. Taylor Corben hired me because she's received some threats against her airline and the resorts. She wants to make sure her guests are kept safe."

Fear plunged a dagger in her heart.

He knows!

This wasn't about him trusting her. He suspected she was a spy and he was testing her. That's was probably why he'd come to her suite last night, but things had heated up between them and he'd gotten distracted.

And she'd allowed it to happen.

The fear escalated into panic. What was she going to say? She was a terrible liar. He'd caught her. She might as well surrender, confess and get it over with.

"Roxie," Dougal's voice broke through her rampant, runaway thoughts.

"Yes?" She trembled.

"You can't tell anyone about this."

She nodded. Everything was ruined. The early euphoria she'd felt fled like sunshine at nightfall. She couldn't have him. There was no hope for salvaging anything between them. She'd betrayed him, and she had to tell Dougal the truth. Never mind that Porter Langley would be disappointed. Never mind that she wouldn't get her promotion or that she'd be out of a job. She could find some other way to get the money for Stacy's college. She could cash in her 401(k). There wasn't much in it, but it might just be enough to pay for her sister's next semester. She could take a second job, a third if necessary, but she couldn't keep lying to Dougal.

In all honesty, she should have already told him. What she'd been doing was wrong and she had to set things right because she was falling in love with him.

Love.

The realization clubbed her. She hadn't been looking for it. Hadn't expected it, but there it was. She was in love with Dougal Lockhart. Her pulse quickened and her gut squeezed miserably.

She was in love with him, and she was about to hurt him as swiftly and as surely as that other woman who'd betrayed his trust and broken his heart.

"Dougal," she said, "there's something very important that I have to tell you, as well."

He went suddenly still. Something in her tone of voice had given her away. "What is it?"

She dragged in a deep breath. "It's a confession really."

He inhaled audibly, and his gaze drilled a hole straight through her. "A confession?"

"I…" Nervously she ran her palms over the tops of her thighs. "I have an ulterior motive for being here."

"And what's that?" he asked.

She swallowed. This was the most difficult news she'd ever had to break to anyone, beyond telling Stacy their parents were never coming home. One sentence and he was never going to look at her the same away again. He'd just spoken of how much he trusted her, and in one breath she was going to take it all away. "This is hard to say."

"Just open your mouth and spit it out."

"I'm not who you think I am."

Dougal looked completely and utterly *crushed*.

"I can explain everything," Roxie said, but Dougal wasn't responding.

"Dougal?" Her voice trembled.

He stared at her as if she was a stranger, his face expressionless. Dougal fisted his hands, a muscle jumped in his jaw, a frown dug deep into his brow. "You're the saboteur." He ground out the words.

Roxie blinked. What was he talking about? "Saboteur?"

He staggered to his feet.

"You." He spat out the word. "You sabotaged the autopilot on the plane."

"What?" She raised a hand to her mouth. Her stomach roiled. *Please don't be sick.* "How would I know how to do something like that?"

"Maybe you had an accomplice. Or maybe the autopilot wasn't part of the sabotage, and it was just a malfunction."

"Huh?"

"You loosened the screws in the stage-light rigging. Anyone could have done it. You wouldn't have to have specialized knowledge."

She gaped at him, unable to believe what he was accusing her of. Speechless, she shook her head.

"You're the one who decapitated the sprinklers. That's a simple matter, as well."

"What?" she repeated dumbly.

"And somehow you infected the computer system with a Trojan."

"I didn't," she whimpered.

His face was pure fury now as he came toward her.

Fear mingled with remorse. She'd never seen him looking so angry. Roxie took three quick steps backward, her retreat halted only by the wall. Her knees locked like rusty hinges.

"Don't lie to me," he said.

"I could never do any of those things," she cried. "I can't believe you think that of me. Dougal, I'm not a saboteur. I swear."

"Then what are you?"

"I'm…" She drew in a heavy breath. "I'm a corporate spy."

He leaned in close, his big body crowding hers. "Who are you working for?"

"Getaway Airlines," she admitted.

"Porter Langley sent you here?"

She nodded. "I wasn't doing it for myself, I was doing it to—"

"You used me."

Roxie stepped toward him, hand outstretched. "It wasn't like that. It was…"

She stopped because what he said was true. Not that she'd slept with him to find out about Eros. By the time they'd made love, she'd forgotten all about the assignment. At that point she'd just been having fun, enjoying her adventure and…*relating everything he told you about Eros right back to Mr. Langley.*

Oh God, it had been exactly like that. Briefly she closed her eyes, knotted her fists. There was no way out of this.

"We have to talk," she said, "and get this straightened out."

"There's nothing to straighten out."

She understood the pain she'd caused him, and it rushed at her dark and hot. There was a hole in her heart, black and empty and guilty, so guilty. Roxie winced, cringed. "I did it for my sister. To get a promotion that would help keep her in college."

"I don't need to hear your excuses. The bottom line is I trusted you." His eyes were hard and dark. He was trying to cloak his feelings, but she could see the hurt simmering in those murky depths. "I told you everything and you didn't come clean with me. You betrayed my trust, Roxie."

Anger shot through her. Yes, she was wrong, but there were two people in this room. She raised her chin defiantly. "I wasn't the only one who was lying. You're not really a tour guide."

"I was undercover. It was my job."

"And I was only doing my job. It's okay for you to deceive me, but it's not okay for me?" She sank her hands on her hips. "That's a double standard if I ever heard one. You just wait for people to slip up so you can crow, 'Oh, I knew I couldn't trust them all along.' You go around with suspicion sitting on your shoulder like Poe's raven, just waiting for someone to make a mistake. But look at your own behavior, Mr. Lockhart. How trustworthy have you been? Sounds like to me that you've got to learn to trust yourself, Dougal. I was wrong, yes, but I did it for the right reasons."

"I guess that's what you have to tell yourself in order to live with what you're doing."

Her anger fled. She was just so sorry things had ended up this way. She'd never wanted to be a spy in the first place. Roxie swallowed. "Dougal, I…please forgive me. I made a big mistake. You've got to forgive me because—"

"I won't be played for a fool, Roxie. I thought we had something special, but now I see we don't."

Then he turned and walked out the door, leaving Roxie to sink down the length of the wall, plant her bottom on the carpet, draw her knees to her chest and sob her heart out.

DOUGAL HARDENED HIS HEART and stalked across the cobble-stones, even as some small part of him whispered, *Forgive.*

Roxie was right after all. He was holding her to a different standard than he held himself. Why was it okay for him to deceive under the guise of his job, but it wasn't okay for her to do the same thing?

He was in the right, dammit! He was protecting Taylor's interests.

His inability to trust had led him here, just as she'd accused. He hadn't really let down his guard with her, he'd only pretended. He'd held part of himself in reserve, waiting for the other shoe to drop and when it had, he'd felt vindicated.

But he sure as hell didn't feel good.

She might be a corporate spy. She might have lied and done some unethical things, but her motives were honest. She was a good person at heart.

Forgive.

His old bullet wound ached. Absentmindedly Dougal rubbed his thigh. Then he hardened his chin and put Roxie out of his mind. He couldn't worry about this now. If she wasn't the saboteur, he had to determine who was.

His cell phone rang. He pulled it from his pocket and checked the caller ID. It was Taylor. "Hello?"

"Dougal," Taylor snapped. "We've got a big problem. Get to a computer. We need to have a video conference call. Now."

AFTER DOUGAL SLAMMED THE DOOR behind him, Roxie admitted the last time she'd felt this lonely, this utterly wretched, was the day she'd learned her parents had been killed. If they could see her now, they'd be so disappointed. The thought ate at her soul.

From the minute she'd agreed to her boss's scheme, she'd known something bad was going to happen. She'd violated her principles, and in doing so, she'd betrayed herself as surely as she'd betrayed Dougal. How could she expect him to forgive her? She couldn't forgive herself. She had knowingly done wrong, even if her motives had been noble.

What was that saying? The road to hell was paved with good intentions.

So what are you going to do about it?

She had to make amends. To herself. To Eros Airlines. To Dougal.

But how?

She needed someone to talk to about what had happened between her and Dougal. She couldn't burden Stacy, but if she just had somebody objective she could tell, it might help her see things more clearly.

Jess and Sam. Yes. That was it. The twins were friendly and upbeat and they weren't personally invested in the outcome. Roxie was certain they could bring a fresh perspective to her dilemma.

Happy to have something to do, somewhere to go and someone to confide in, Roxie picked herself up off the floor and went in search of the twins.

14

"What's up?" Dougal asked Taylor when they had the video conference call connected. She looked royally pissed off, but she'd refused to tell him what had her so upset. She said she wanted him to see for himself.

"I want you to go to this blog," Taylor said and gave him the Internet address.

Dougal tapped it in, and a second later up popped a blog with the headline: Our Eros Vacation. On the right side was a photograph of Jess and Sam.

"What am I looking for?' Dougal asked as he started reading the blog.

"Scroll down."

He did and more photographs popped into view, photographs not of the twin sisters, but of him and Roxie. There was one of them kissing in the punt. It looked as if it had been snapped from above, as if Sam and Jess had lain in wait on one of the bridges on the Cam to catch them at exactly the wrong moment. There was a picture of them climbing down the belltower steps together, holding hands. Another photograph depicted Dougal and Roxie onstage when they'd recited the sonnet together, their lips mere inches apart. But it was the last photograph that killed his soul. It was a shot of him and Roxie leaving the dungeon together, their clothes askew, their faces flushed, and he was looking at Roxie with such love on his face that a blind man could have seen his feelings for her.

Beside the photographs were snarky little captions all designed to draw attention to the fact that an Eros tour guide was behaving inappropriately with a guest of the resort.

"I'm so sorry, Taylor."

"Who is this woman?"

"She's a spy for Porter Langley," Dougal said.

"Is she the same person who has been sabotaging my resorts?"

"No."

"Well I gotta tell you, Dougal." Taylor ran a hand through her hair. "This feels just the same as sabotage."

"I'm truly sorry, Taylor. Of course I will give you back your fee," he said. "I not only didn't do my job, but I exhibited unprofessional behavior."

"That's not necessary. I just wanted to know if you were okay. After what happened in Germany, this must be a blow to discover the woman you're in love with is a corporate spy who was just using you."

The pain in his chest stabbed fresh and sharp. "I'm not in love with her," he denied.

"Oh, Dougal, you don't have to lie to me."

His shoulders slumped, his heart slid to his feet. "It's that obvious?"

"If I could, I'd reach out and give you a big hug."

He snorted. "It was my own stupidity."

"Are you sure she doesn't feel anything for you?"

He shook his head. "I'm not sure of anything anymore, Taylor."

"May I give you a piece of advice from someone who denied love for too long?"

He shrugged. "If you think it will help."

"Go to her, tell her how you feel. Even if she doesn't feel the same way, it's better to know where you stand than to keep forever guessing."

"AND THAT'S THE WHOLE sordid story," Roxie said to Jess and Sam after she'd related everything that had happened.

They were all submerged in a bubbly hot tub just off the lobby of the resort, underneath a pergola.

"Wow," Sam said, "that's some tale."

"I would never have taken you for a spy," Jess added.

Roxie thought confessing her sins to the twins would make her feel better, but it had not. On the contrary, she was more miserable than ever and no closer to a solution.

Sam lifted a glass of wine to her lips. "I think—" She broke off and her eyes widened.

"Um, oh," Jess said, staring in the same direction as her sister.

Roxie swiveled her head to see what had captured the twins' attention.

It was Dougal. Stalking straight toward them and glowering darkly.

Thrill at the sight of him and fear at the fierce displeasure in his eyes squeezed Roxie's heart. What had she done now?

Jess and Sam were suddenly scrambling out of the hot tub, grabbing for their bathrobes and towels. They looked supremely guilty.

What was going on?

"Hey," Dougal said, breaking into a trot. "Stop right there, you two."

"Um…" Jess raised a hand, sent him a dazzling smile. "Hi, Dougal."

"Don't give me that," Dougal barked, his long legs taking him to the edge of the hot tub. He never even glanced in Roxie's direction. "I know what you've been up to."

Confused by the turn of events, Roxie slogged from the water. Feeling extremely exposed, she reached for her own robe, pulled it over her one-piece bathing suit and belted it at the waist. She glanced from Dougal to the twins and back again.

"You ambushed me and Roxie. Took compromising pictures of us and posted them on the Internet," he accused.

Jess and Sam looked sheepish.

Befuddled, Roxie pushed her damp hair off her face and tried to understand what he was saying.

"Who hired you to sabotage Eros?" Dougal demanded.

Jess and Sam were the saboteurs? Roxie's mouth dropped open.

"You did something to disrupt the autopilot on the Eros jet," Dougal continued. "You loosened the stage lighting so it would fall. You destroyed the sprinklers—"

"Whoa, hey." Sam held up her palms. "Wait just a darn minute. We're not involved in anything like that."

Dougal's scowl deepened. "Then what are you involved in?"

Jess darted a nervous glance toward Roxie and wet her lips. "Um, could we have this discussion in private?"

For the first time since he'd arrived, Dougal looked at Roxie. His expression was unreadable, but she was getting weird vibes from both him and the twins. "What is going on?" she demanded.

"We might as well just tell her," Sam said to her sister. "She's going to find out."

"Tell me what?" Roxie's bare feet chilled against the red-wood decking, but it wasn't so much from the cool springtime air as from the discussion.

Jess shifted her weight but didn't meet Roxie's eyes. "Because," she told Dougal, "we were playing matchmaker."

"Matchmaker?" Dougal and Roxie said in unison.

"We got you to take us on the punt, and then we arranged for Mike and David to show up so we could force you and Dougal to be alone together," Sam said.

"In a romantic venue," Jess added. "And under titillating circumstances."

"But why would you do that?" Roxie asked.

Jess slid her twin a look. Sam nodded, giving her the go-ahead. "Porter Langley hired us to make sure Roxie had an affair with one of the Eros staff members."

"And it worked," Sam pointed out.

"What?" Stunned by what they'd just admitted, Roxie could only stare.

"You had an affair with him." Jess jerked her head toward Dougal.

"I don't get it." Roxie felt lost. "Porter sent me here to gather insider information on Eros."

"That's just what he told you," Sam said. "In actuality, he was using you as a pawn."

"Wait." Dougal sank his hands on his hips. "Now I'm confused. What exactly is Porter Langley up to?"

"Here's how he explained it to us," Jess put in. "He wanted to create a scandal for Eros. His plan was to send Roxie on the Romance of Britannia tour as a corporate spy. His real play was to capitalize on her inexperience in romantic relationships and use it to bring down Taylor Corben."

"To that end—" Sam picked up the story "—he hired us. We're private investigators, specializing in tempting cheating husbands to make passes at us so their wives have grounds for divorce."

"That's entrapment," Dougal growled.

Jess shrugged. "We make a very good living."

"Actually," Sam said, "that's how we met Porter. He tried to pick us up for a threesome."

Roxie couldn't believe what she was hearing. "But why would you do this to me?"

"To get proof that Eros employees are having sex with the guests."

Roxie's breath fled her lungs. "What? And how were you going to prove this?"

"We're very good at our jobs," Jess said. "You should be

careful what you do in semipublic places." She shook her head. "And telephoto lenses are quite the modern miracle."

Roxie felt as if she'd been kicked in the gut. "You...you have pictures?"

"Yes, and we already posted them to our Web site," Sam confirmed.

Roxie's head swirled. Her boss had used her, and these women who she'd thought were her friends had betrayed her. The enormity of what had happened washed over Roxie. Not only had her stupidity got her into trouble, but she'd put Dougal's job in jeopardy, as well. "But I trusted you."

"That was your first mistake." Sam held up her palms.

"You should be ashamed of yourselves," Dougal snarled and fisted his hands.

"No," Jess countered, "you should be ashamed of yourself. Having sex with a guest." She clicked her tongue. "You broke the rules, Dougal, and now you're going to have to deal with the consequences."

NO WORDS COULD DESCRIBE the savage despair churning inside him.

He was angry, yes. Worried, most assuredly. But even though those emotions were strong, they weren't primary. No, the main sensation raging inside him was the urge to protect Roxie at all costs.

One look at her face told him the whole story. She was hurt beyond measure. Questioning herself, doubting her ability to read people. He knew what she was feeling, because he'd been there. He'd felt her pain.

"Roxie." He called her name without knowing what else he was going to say. He reached for her, but she was in no state of mind to turn to him. With jerky movements she stepped back, arms raised.

"Roxie," he called.

"Leave me alone. Please, just leave me alone." She ducked her head and ran away, her bare feet pattering against the tiles.

Glaring, he turned to Jess and Sam. "Are you proud of yourselves? You've hurt one of the finest women I've ever known."

"Hey," Jess said, "we were only doing a job. It was nothing personal."

"Destroying someone is always personal," he growled. "Her career will be ruined, her reputation in shambles."

Sam defiantly lifted her chin. "In that case, you should accept responsibility for your role in Roxie's downfall."

Her words sliced him clean through the bone. She was right. If he'd been a stronger man, more in control of his desires, this never would have happened. He'd failed Roxie and he'd failed himself.

FEELING HUMILIATED OVER the knowledge that her tryst had been caught on camera and that her boss had hired Jess and Sam to manufacture a romance between her and Dougal to bring scandal to Eros, Roxie fled to her room. She got out of her bathing suit and put on some clothes.

You'll get through this, she tried to reassure herself, but she felt so lost and alone. And all she could think about was Dougal. How she'd violated her own moral code by agreeing to spy on Eros for her boss, and in the process, she'd inadvertently betrayed Dougal.

But he'd betrayed her, too. He'd thought she was a saboteur. He'd been nice to her, romanced her, when in reality he'd been trying to get her to trip up. Roxie didn't believe that he'd made love to her to get her to confess. On that score she truly did believe he'd simply been as swept away by their chemistry as she'd been. She curled her hands into fists, her fingernails biting into her palms.

What she needed was something to stop her mind from whirling. A distraction. A physical outlet. A run, a swim... That's when she realized she'd paused outside the resort's gymnasium. Apparently her subconscious had brought her here. She read the activities offered on the menu outside the door. Aerobics classes, Pilates, free weights, a fencing area.

Fencing.

Yes, yes. A good fencing workout was exactly what she needed, but the posted hours said the gym was closed after noon on Sundays. Dammit.

In frustration, she grabbed the door handle, intending on shaking it just to let off some steam, but to her surprise the door opened. Someone had forgotten to lock up.

The lights were out in the gym, but the big picture window provided more than enough light. Furtively she glanced around. The corridor was empty. Smiling, she stepped into the gym as the door whispered closed behind her.

"GO TO HER, TELL HER HOW you feel. Even if she doesn't feel the same way, it's better to know where you stand than to keep forever guessing."

Taylor's words rang in his ears.

How could he be in love with Roxie? He'd only known her two short weeks. And yet his heart ached in an odd way it had never ached before. He had to tell her...what?

He had no idea what he was going to say. He just knew he had to talk to her.

He went to her room, banged on the door, but she didn't answer. Finally he flashed his badge and asked a maid to let him into her room.

It was empty.

The twinge in his heart tightened. Where was she?

Dougal searched the resort. She wasn't in the any of the restaurants or bars, nor was she hidden away in an alcove. No Roxie in the lobby or the swimming pool area or the business office. He interviewed the valets, who swore that no one matching her description had left the resort. He almost skipped over the gym because it was closed on Sunday afternoons, but as he passed the door he heard the unmistakable sound of adept footwork, accompanied by the noise of a dueling sword slicing through the air.

Gotcha.

Grinning, he pushed open the door.

Roxie's back was to him, and she was in the middle of battling an imaginary opponent with her foil. She wore no fencing gear. Immediately his eyes were drawn to the flexing movements of her sweet little fanny encased in a pair of formfitting slacks.

"En garde," he murmured.

She whirled around, her weapon at the ready. Although she didn't wear a fencing mask, her expression was unreadable. Her eyes lit on his as she struck the basic advance pose. *"En garde."*

He glanced to the rack where the dueling weapons lay. He stalked over, picked out a foil, unsheathed it and turned to square off with her.

Without a word, she stamped her front foot to the ground, producing a sound known as an appel. The intention was to startle him. He anticipated the lunge, raised his foil to meet hers, gliding it down her blade, keeping her in constant contact.

Dougal had never fenced without gear. For a man who was always braced for trouble, it felt strange being so unprepared for battle, but oddly calming.

"Are you okay?" he asked.

She executed an interesting little maneuver called a ballestra lunge that was a lunge, feint, lunge combo that almost made him lose his footing. "Don't worry about me."

"I can't help it," he said, regaining his balance and coming at her before she could mount a fresh attack. "I know what it's like to be on the receiving end of a betrayal."

"Have you ever considered," she asked, "that you set yourself up for betrayal?"

"Excuse me?"

"You expect people to let you down and so they usually do. I've discovered that when you treat people as if they are trustworthy, they generally are." Their blades clanged loudly in the high ceiling gym.

"Oh yeah, just like Jess and Sam and your boss were trustworthy."

"Yes, they betrayed me. Yes, I was gullible and naive and too trusting. But you know what? That's my own fault."

"For placing your trust in others." Dougal nodded.

"No," Roxie said, her face deadly earnest as she rounded on him with a new lunge. "For not getting out there and experiencing things before now. I used raising Stacy as an excuse to hide from life. I was afraid of being hurt, so I never let myself love anyone other than my little sister."

Her swordplay was aggressive, her expression fierce. They went back and forth, thrust, parry, thrust, parry.

"You on the other hand…"

"Yeah?"

"You distrust people as a way to avoid pain."

"Excuse me?"

"Distrust is your modus operandi. Your fallback position."

"Is that so?"

"If you assume people can't be trusted, then you can't ever be truly disappointed."

He lunged, causing her to retreat down the fencing strip. "And where did you get your degree in psychology?"

"Ooh, sarcasm. Another defense mechanism for the disillusioned," she retorted.

She was right but he was loath to admit it. "You do understand the real problem, don't you?"

"I'm positive you're about to enlighten me."

"It wasn't until I found out about Jess and Sam working for Porter Langley that I got it."

Okay, fine, she'd piqued his curiosity. "Got what?"

"You don't trust other people because you don't fully trust yourself."

"I'm missing the connection," he said.

"I trusted too much. I thought other people would be like me. Open, honest, caring. So that made me think that you're distrustful because you expect people to be like you."

"Huh?"

"It's a paradox, I know. But until you allow yourself to be open and vulnerable, then you'll never be able to fully trust your instincts or other people." Her blade tipped lightly against his shoulder. It was only when he felt the air against his skin that he realized she'd cut through the sleeve of his flannel shirt.

"Touché," Dougal croaked.

"Like it or not, I get you."

He did like it, and *that's* what he didn't like.

Her swordplay sent him backward. She scored another point on his other sleeve, and then did a crazy little ripple with her foil. Suddenly she'd cut off his shirt. The garment fluttered to the ground in shredded pieces, revealing his bare chest.

Their gazes locked. Lust shot through him sharp as her sword. How he wanted her!

Roxie came at him again. Dougal was on the defensive and he was unlikely to recover. She was a much better fencer than he, with far superior control and understanding of the finer points of engagement. She took him off the fencing strip and into a corner. He would already have lost in match play. His back was literally to the wall. He had nowhere to go.

If he had any hope of walking away unscathed from his encounter with her, it was now or never. Dougal lunged toward her at maximum thrust, desperately seeking to regain control, but Roxie smoothly sidestepped, simultaneously wielding her foil in a swift maneuver and disarmed him.

His sword clattered to the floor.

He was doomed.

Roxie's smile was wicked, and it filled him with a kind of happiness he'd never felt before. It was the kind of feeling that altered a man in every way possible.

"I see you for who you are, Dougal Lockhart," she murmured. "I know what's got you twisted up inside."

He stood there, fully exposed, vulnerable, his chest rising and falling rapidly as he sucked air into his lungs.

She raised her blade.

Dougal gulped, lifted his arms over his head in the universal gesture of surrender.

Then with a blindly swift motion, she sliced open the leg of his jeans right at the level of his scar. With the gentlest of a feather-soft caress, she touched her blade to his ravaged skin and whispered, "Do you trust me?"

DOUGAL NEVER TOOK HIS GAZE off her face. "I trust you," he said, and she could tell he meant every word.

Roxie dropped the foil.

He wrapped his arms around her, squeezed her as if he was never going to let her go. Then his lips were on hers and everything that had driven her to this moment made perfect sense.

Roxie twined her arms around his neck, and for the longest time they just kissed. She couldn't get enough of his touch, his taste, his smell. He was in her blood, in her heart, and she knew she could never get him out.

Finally they had to come up for air.

"I'm not sure what this thing is, sweetheart—" he began.

"We don't have to define it."

He placed a finger to her lips. "Listen to me for a minute." She quieted, watching his face.

"You're right about me. Deep down, I don't trust myself. I'm always afraid I'm going to make a mistake and someone is going to suffer because of me. But with you, because of you…" He took a deep breath. "Roxie, I think we could have something really great."

She gulped, overcome by emotion. "I do, too."

"It's probably too soon to say the word *love*…but you're right. I've got to allow myself to be vulnerable or I'll never be able to trust myself. I'm scared as hell, I'm going out on a limb here and I'm saying it. Roxanne Stanley, I think I'm falling in love with you."

"Oh, Dougal," she sighed, filled with so much joy and happiness she could hardly speak. "I think I'm falling in love with you, too."

Epilogue

"YOU HAVE THE JOB IF YOU want it," Taylor Corben said. "But only under one condition."

Roxie drew herself up to her full five-foot-six height. She desperately needed this job after telling off Porter Langley and walking away from Getaway Airlines, but there were a few things she just wouldn't do.

"What's the condition?" she asked.

Taylor jerked a thumb to Dougal, who was leaning insouciantly against the wall on one shoulder, his arms crossed over his chest. "Keep doing whatever it is you've been doing to this guy. I've never seen him so happy."

Roxie thought of everything they'd been doing during the two weeks they'd been back in the States—making love, picnicking in Central Park, making love, walking hand in hand through the Museum of Art, making love, taking in a few Broadway plays, making love, meeting each other's friends and families, making love. "That's not a hard promise to keep."

"Pun intended I hope," Taylor teased. "But seriously, Roxie, I'm glad to have you aboard."

"I'm just so happy you gave me a chance after I spied on your operation for Getaway."

"Are you kidding? Good executive assistants are worth

their weight in gold. And even though you told him to get stuffed, Porter Langley gave you a glowing recommendation."

"His conscience must have got the best of him." Roxie smiled.

"And don't worry, I won't ask you to do anything that goes against your moral code."

"Thank you."

"About your starting salary…" Taylor said, and named a figure that was one and a half times what Langley had been paying her. "You'll be getting a raise at the end of your three-month probationary period, of course. I hope that's satisfactory."

"Very satisfactory." Roxie couldn't help shooting a look of triumph over at Dougal. He looked so handsome. Her man.

Her man.

The words warmed her up inside.

"Wonderful." Taylor leaned across the desk to shake Roxie's hand. "Welcome to Eros Airlines."

"Thank you."

Taylor turned her attention to Dougal. "So no word on the saboteur?"

He shook his head. "We were unable to conclusively tie any of the occurrences on the Romance of Britannia tour together. My men report there've been no problems at any of the other resorts. I'm beginning to think those threatening letters are just that—empty threats."

Taylor nodded but she didn't look placated. Just then her cell phone rang. She raised a finger for Dougal and Roxie to excuse her as she took the call. They got up to leave, but Taylor suddenly motioned them to stay. She listened to the caller, and then said, "Do it."

She hung up the phone and looked at Dougal, her face noticeably pale.

"What is it?" Dougal asked.

Taylor swallowed "They found a bomb in the lobby of our Japanese resort. Looks like those threats aren't so empty after all."

* * * * *

Don't miss award-winning Lori Wilde's
next sexy romance in her latest miniseries,
HIS FINAL SEDUCTION,
coming in January 2010
from Harlequin Blaze®!

Celebrate 60 years of pure reading pleasure
with Harlequin®!
Just in time for the holidays,
Silhouette Special Edition® is proud to present
New York Times *bestselling author*
Kathleen Eagle's
ONE COWBOY, ONE CHRISTMAS

Rodeo rider Zach Beaudry was a travelin' man—until he
broke down in middle-of-nowhere South Dakota during
a deep freeze. That's when an angel came to his rescue....

underneath that silk.

"Don't die on me. Come on, Zel. You know how much I love you, girl. You're all I've got. Don't do this to me here. Not *now*."

But Zelda had quit on him, and Zach Beaudry had no one to blame but himself. He'd taken his sweet time hitting the road, and then miscalculated a shortcut. For all he knew he was a hundred miles from gas. But even if they were sitting next to a pump, the ten dollars he had in his pocket wouldn't get him out of South Dakota, which was not where he wanted to be right now. Not even his beloved pickup truck, Zelda, could get him much of anywhere on fumes. He was sitting out in the cold in the middle of nowhere. And getting colder.

He shifted the pickup into Neutral and pulled hard on the steering wheel, using the downhill slope to get her off the blacktop and into the roadside grass, where she shuddered to a standstill. He stroked the padded dash. "You'll be safe here."

But Zach would not. It was getting dark, and it was already too damn cold for his cowboy ass. Zach's battered body was a barometer, and he was feeling South Dakota, big-time. He'd have given his right arm to be climbing into a hotel hot tub instead of a brutal blast of north wind. The right was his free arm anyway. Damn thing had lost altitude, touched some part of the bull and caused him a scoreless ride last time out.

It wasn't scoring him a ride this night, either. A carload of teenagers whizzed by, topping off the insult by laying on the horn as they passed him. It was at least twenty minutes before another vehicle came along. He stepped out and waved both arms this time, damn near getting himself killed. Whatever happened to *do unto others?* In places like this, decent people didn't leave each other stranded in the cold.

His face was feeling stiff, and he figured he'd better start walking before his toes went numb. He struck out for a distant yard light, the only sign of human habitation in sight. He couldn't tell how distant, but he knew he'd be hurting by the time he got there, and he was counting on some kindly old man to be answering the door. No shame among the lame.

It wasn't like Zach was fresh off the operating table—it had been a few months since his last round of repairs—but he hadn't given himself enough time. He'd lopped a couple of weeks off the near end of the doc's estimated recovery time, rigged up a brace, done some heavy-duty taping and climbed onto another bull. Hung in there for five seconds—four seconds past feeling the pop in his hip and three seconds short of the buzzer.

He could still feel the pain shooting down his leg with every step. Only this time he had to pick the damn thing up, swing it forward and drop it down again on his own.

Pride be damned, he just hoped *somebody* would be answering the door at the end of the road. The light in the front window was a good sign.

The four steps to the covered porch might as well have been four hundred, and he was looking to climb them with a lead weight chained to his left leg. His eyes were just as screwed up as his hip. Big black spots danced around with tiny red flashers, and he couldn't tell what was real and what wasn't. He stumbled over some shrubbery, steadied himself on the porch railing and peered between vertical slats.

There in the front window stood a spruce tree with a silver star affixed to the top. Zach was pretty sure the red sparks were all in his head, but the white lights twinkling by the hundreds throughout the huge tree, those were real. He wasn't too sure about the woman hanging the shiny balls. Most of her hair was caught up on her head and fastened in a curly clump, but the light captured by the escaped bits crowned her with a golden halo. Her face was a soft shadow, her body a willowy silhouette beneath a long white gown. If this was where the mind ran off to when cold started shutting down the rest of the body, then Zach's final worldly thought was, *This ain't such a bad way to go.*

If she would just turn to the window, he could die looking into the eyes of a Christmas angel.

* * * * *

Could this woman from Zach's past
get the lonesome cowboy to come in
from the cold…for good?
Look for
ONE COWBOY, ONE CHRISTMAS
by Kathleen Eagle.
Available December 2009
from Silhouette Special Edition®.

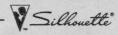

SPECIAL EDITION

We're spotlighting
a different series
every month throughout 2009
to celebrate our 60th anniversary.

This December, Silhouette Special Edition® brings you

NEW YORK TIMES BESTSELLING AUTHOR

KATHLEEN EAGLE

ONE COWBOY, ONE CHRISTMAS

Available wherever books are sold.

Silhouette *Desire*

**FROM *NEW YORK TIMES*
BESTSELLING AUTHOR**

DIANA
PALMER

THE MAVERICK

A BRAND-NEW
LONG, TALL
TEXAN STORY

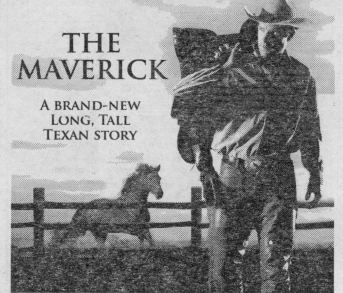

Visit Silhouette Books at www.eHarlequin.com

SD76982

REQUEST YOUR FREE BOOKS!

2 FREE NOVELS PLUS 2 FREE GIFTS!

HARLEQUIN®

Blaze™

Red-hot reads!

HB09R3

COMING NEXT MONTH
Available November 24, 2009

#507 BETTER NAUGHTY THAN NICE Vicki Lewis Thompson, Jill Shalvis, Rhonda Nelson
A Blazing Holiday Collection
Bad boy Damon Claus is determined to mess things up for his jolly big brother, Santa. Who'd ever guess that sibling rivalry would result in mistletoe madness for three unsuspecting couples! And Damon didn't even have to spike the eggnog....

#508 STARSTRUCK Julie Kenner
For Alyssa Chambers, having the perfect Christmas means snaring the perfect man. And she has him all picked out. Too bad it's her best friend, Christopher Hyde, who has her seeing stars.

#509 TEXAS BLAZE Debbi Rawlins
The Wrong Bed
Hot and heavy. That's how Kate Manning and Mitch Colter have always been for each other. But it's not till Kate makes the right move—though technically in the wrong bed—that things start heating up for good!

#510 SANTA, BABY Lisa Renee Jones
Dressed to Thrill, Bk. 4
As a blonde bombshell, Caron Avery thinks she's got enough attitude to bring a man to his knees. But when she seduces hot playboy Baxter Remington, will she be the one begging for more?

#511 CHRISTMAS MALE Cara Summers
Uniformly Hot!
All policewoman Fiona Gallagher wants for Christmas is a little excitement. But once she finds herself working on a case with sexy captain D. C. Campbell, she's suddenly aching for a different kind of thrill....

#512 TWELVE NIGHTS Hope Tarr
Blaze Historicals
Lady Alys is desperately in love with Scottish bad boy Callum Fraser. And keeping him out of her bed until the wedding is nearly killing her. So what's stopping them from indulging? Uhh...Elys's deceased first husband, a man very much alive.